Ahoy Daddy!
Pride Cruise 2024 Series
TL Travis

Sapphire Publishing

Disclaimer

Many of the challenges Vale faces in this story are ones I contend with daily and have to work past.

The diagnosis at four, negative reactions to the meds, and yes, even drinking coffee since the age of the first hyperactivity diagnosis turned ADHD is all me.

Our ADHD-riddled minds are just that—our own, and how they react and what they are driven by and respond to varies by each person. Mistaking our drive and focus as cockiness is an unfair assumption because for many of us it's a coping mechanism, a way to talk ourselves off the proverbial ledge.

We have processes in place within our daily lives to complete the simplest of tasks. We blurt things out unfiltered though we try to resist, at least I do. We do the best we can even though our minds are going a million miles a minute, always on the next tasks that lie ahead. At times the responses we give aren't to your questions but to ones our brains are currently tackling.

The point is each ADHD or neurodivergent diagnosis is different. Each coping mechanism, whether it be written lists, spreadsheets, or something such as fidget spinners, are a necessity for us. And while I repeatedly use the words "us" and "we" in this disclaimer, in this case I mean me.

So please, when reading this story keep an open mind and be aware that not all of us operate the in the same manner.

Always be kind to others. You don't know what challenges or demons they face.

Contents

Chapter One
Vale

"Are you sure you want to do this? It's not too late to back out, you know." My mom pleaded with me for the millionth time, unable to hide her fear of the ocean. And boats. And really water in general. Sometimes it amazed me that she showered. It was justified, though, her fear that was. At least in my eyes and hers, but I'd already signed on, completed the training, and would see this through.

Now, whether my new job as a cabin steward panned out or not would be the true test.

Gods of the sea, give me the strength to not be me.

"Yes, Mom." Good lord, would she ever get over this? I understood her fear, having watched me nearly drown when I was four. But whereas that drove me to become the best swimmer I could be, it only pushed her further back in the healing process. The poor woman was beside herself since I'd made the decision to join the crew of the cruise ship Magdalena, thanks to my best and really only friend, Darcy, who was a chief cabin steward aboard the ship.

Given the fact I'd spent my first few days of training in the infirmary with motion sickness, that only made matters worse in her eyes. But for me, once I got my sea legs it was smooth sailing from then on out.

He–he, smooth sailing. I crack myself up.

"Mom, you deserve a break and I need a job. This is a win–win for both of us." I hoped. Fuck, if I was wrong I'd be totally screwed and stuck in the middle of the ocean with no way out.

"You're my baby boy and I don't need a break from you, nor have I ever considered you a burden. We're a team, you and me. I don't want you to go, especially not where you're off to." She dared not say *boat* or *ship* or any water vessel for that matter for fear of cursing the trip. "I do understand you're an adult and make your own decisions, but it doesn't mean I have to like them."

Did she truly understand, though? Hmm, the jury was still deliberating.

She spoke *her* truth, though. Mom would never give me anything but that. She always said, "We may not have a lot of money or at times any, but we always stay true to our word and earn what we have." The woman was wise beyond her years.

My inability to sleep all night, nor nap, had plagued the poor woman since I came running out of her womb and right into the waiting world. Diagnosed with hyperactivity at the young age of four, then as an adult with ADHD, she'd never had a break. We'd tried every medication known, whether prescription or holistic, and nothing worked but coffee. Even that was minimal at best.

Yes, I've been drinking coffee since I was four. Don't shame me.

For all intents and purposes, I was just...me. Or as Mom preferred to say, I was unique. My own person and her special little man.

Unique, special, with an uncanny knack to drive every human I encountered insane within the first hour of meeting me, except for Darcy. Don't get me wrong, there were times she wanted to choke me, but she was still there for me. *Always.*

Keep a job? That was near impossible, and my extensive resume spoke to that. Had to remove quite a few failed attempts to make it work without overwhelming potential employers. No one would read a twenty-seven-page resume. Not that mine was that long, but you get the gist of it.

Lack of focus ✓
Talk too much ✓
Acts on impulse ✓ ✓
Yeah...

Imagine trying to keep a boyfriend.

Not. Gonna. Happen.

I was doomed to lead a lonely life so I might as well have as much fun as I could, even if it was by myself.

When the one friend I'd somehow managed to keep suggested I join her crew, it was something I had to seriously consider. As much as it pained me to think about, Mom wasn't going to be here forever. Besides, it was time I became a fully functioning adult.

And now here I was, boarding the cruise ship in Seattle at the butt crack of dawn for a just over two week, all gay Pride Cruise.

May the gods of the sea shine brightly upon me.

Or something along those lines...

Either way, it should be interesting. Right?

"Vale! Vale!"

Darcy called out to me, already on board, her arms frantically waving as she struggled to gain my attention. "You nearly missed check-in."

"I know. I forgot to finish packing, then crammed everything into my luggage this morning. Then made the mistake of stopping for coffee and left right after I paid for it so I had to turn around and pick it up." Idiot brain. When it kept focused I did amazing things. Knocked tasks off my lists like a champ. But when my focus was shit, all hell broke loose and the simplest of things slipped through the cracks.

Without any sort of outlet or goals set.

Fucking squirrels.

With the cabin steward job, Darcy had check-lists with our daily tasks for us to work from and we had a limited amount of time to spend in each cabin to complete them. Organized chaos was how I best operated and this sounded like the ideal job for me.

She met me at check-in and led me to the room I had been assigned. I hoped my room-mate wasn't... "Wait." Darcy opened the door and her silly familiar rainbow teddy bear blankie sat at the foot of one of the beds. Given how many times we'd curled up together under it while watching movies, there was no mis-taking it. "How'd you swing this?" To say I was relieved didn't even cover it.

"I have my ways," she winked. "Given your openness in answering the employee questionnaire, I asked if it would be possible to have you as a roommate and Captain Solis agreed."

"Thank the gay gods for that. I was so afraid of a less ADHD-tolerant roommate getting stuck with me."

"That and the fact we're both gay gave him less pause for concern. There are some on the crew that are actual couples and long-time employees, and he allows them to share a room. With us being BFFs it was an easy sell. Come on, let's get you unpacked. We're in this tin can far too long to live out of suitcases."

Darcy and the other chief cabin stewards boarded yesterday to verify the previous team had set all the rooms right. What wasn't done, they fixed and prepared for the newbies to on-board today. Later this afternoon the passengers would join us. Then the chaos would begin.

Thanks to Darcy, my things were put away in record time and we were off to meet the others for a quick crew meeting the captain had called in the conference center before the passengers boarded. Promptly at the top of the hour, Captain Solis's face appeared on the big screen and his booming voice silenced the rowdy crowd.

"Welcome, both new and returning crew members. As we embark upon this sixteen-day voyage to the Hawaiian Islands, I felt it prudent to point out that we will be hosting a sold-out crowd." Claps and cheers erupted. "Yes, yes, we will be busy for sure and with that many bodies aboard, as much as we could hope and pray for smooth sailing, it won't be without hiccups. Therefore, we've increased security presence." Gentle head bobs rolled through the room in a sinuous wave. Mostly by returning staff who must've experienced these types of challenges previously.

"Please turn to the secondary monitor to review our itinerary." Captain Solis read it aloud.

"Day 1, Seattle, set sail at 4pm sharp."

"Days 2, 3, 4, 5, 6 - all at sea."

Whoa, that is a long time...

"Day 7 - Honolulu, Oahu."

"Day 8 - Nawiliwili, Kaui."

"Day 9 - Kahului, Maui."

"Day 10 - Hilo, Hawaii."

"Days 11, 12, 13, 14 - all at sea."

"Day 15 - Victoria, BC."

"Day 16 - Seattle."

Would I be able to survive this?

Suddenly, the length of my contract slapped me upside the head. Four months. In one place. With no escape.

Wasn't this how most horror movies began?

"As you'll note, there are many consecutive days spent at sea and given that this is a themed cruise, the passengers will get restless and it's up to you to redirect their attention when you spot changes in attitude and actions. Mention the casino, the pools, shopping, etc. Since it's a kink cruise, remind them of the dungeon, littles' playroom, or even the pet play area."

Pet play?

I nearly yanked my phone from my pocket to open the map of the ship that I'd saved, which would've reflected poorly on me. This was something I'd surely remember once the meeting ended without being rude. But I wanted to see which room the animals would be in. *Pet play.* The words rolled around in my head. I planned to spend as much of my free time there as possible. Animals had a calming effect on me, but I didn't know we allowed non-assistance animals on-board.

But puppies?

Yes, please.

After the meeting adjourned, the steward staff returned to their designated areas to await any incoming calls from guests as they settled into their cabins and suites. Extra towels were the most asked for. We were given our list of cabin assignments and when the phones started ringing, we were off and running for sixteen fun-filled days of non-stop work.

Yes, you heard that right. Ten-to-fourteen-hour daily shifts for the duration of the cruise.

Good thing I wasn't a sleeper.

In between calls, we took the time to introduce ourselves to as many of the guests in our assigned areas as possible. Only made sense since we were already on the floor fulfilling their requests, though some had already wandered off and weren't in their rooms when I stopped by.

"Good afternoon, my name is Vale and I'll be your cabin steward for the duration of your journey." One by one I checked in at each cabin in the thirty-five units I was assigned. When I got to the last one my achy feet and I were ready for a break.

The door opened right as I knocked, and the man inside barreled into me. Prepared to land on my ass, imagine my surprise when I didn't.

"I'm so sorry." His arms held me in place. "I'm Vale, your..."

"My what?"

I nearly forgot where I was when he smiled. "Your-your..." Words escaped me just by being in this handsome man's presence.

"Steward?" he replied for me. I managed to nod as he helped me stand.

"Yes. Your steward. Vale. Hello, I'm Steward. I'm Vale." *Ridiculous. Way to make a fool of yourself.*

"Wonderful to meet you, Vale." Again, with that smile. Had I ever been stunned by a man as I was with him?

The answer was unequivocally no.

"Okay. Bye." I bolted down the hall, right to the stairway, and didn't stop until I reached my cabin.

"Why are you so out of breath?" Darcy asked. She knew better than to panic before I explained whatever mayhem I had gotten into. Having dealt with a mistake or a thousand of mine over the years, she didn't easily rile.

"Man. Fell. Hot." I slid to the floor behind the door, and she handed me a bottle of water.

"Deep breaths." My dear friend had the patience of a saint. "Okay, now start from the beginning."

"I got to my last room, right as I went to knock the door opened and the guy ran into me. Nearly knocked me on my ass but he caught me and just held me there. His cologne was so musky. He was so…" and I chased the squirrel down a path I dare not tread but damn, was it sweet.

"Do. Not. Go. There. Vale. You know the rules."

I did and Darcy went to bat for me with this job. My employment track record was less than stellar but she pushed, and they hired me. "I know." But that smile would be tucked away as a happy place for me.

She took my hand and helped me up. "Come on, let's get dinner."

The day had flown by, and it was later than I thought when we reached the employee dining area. With a staff head count well into the hundreds, the dining hall operated twenty-four hours a day with two shifts. Surprisingly, the café boasted a large menu to choose from and the food wasn't bad.

"Now, the real fun begins," Darcy said as we took a seat. "The one positive on these voyages is that we're never bored and work so hard we pass out as soon as our heads hit the pillows. You might actually sleep, Vale."

"Funny girl." But one could only hope.

"All right, eat up so we can give the remaining members of our team their dinner break."

"Wait, there's more work?" Whining wasn't me but damn, my feet hurt. While sharing a room had many perks, the long hours that would come with it might just do me in.

"Yes, my youngling. There is so much more. The night is young, as are we and the boat is packed. Welcome to the crew."

Part of the crew, part of the team. How those infamous words rattled my brain.

With a quick finger comb to my wavy hair, not much else I could do with it, we were off and running. Literally. Until the overnight crew took over.

"Is it always like this?" Darcy and I had just returned to our room for the night, both well beyond exhausted. Young or not, running like we were had worn out my hyper ass, and that was saying something.

"Pretty much. When the passengers go ashore for island excursions, it's quiet call wise but we're usually cleaning their rooms so we're still busy. But free room and board plus we still get paid. Four months on with a month off. For me, that makes it worth it. I crash at my mom's when I'm home, meanwhile my income sits in the bank earning interest. Until I find my forever person, this is the life for me."

Also, the way Darcy avoided heartbreak. Again.

Wasn't that what it all came down to? Buying into the dream that our forever awaited us somewhere out in the great wide unknown. As humans, we hold onto that dream in the hopes our aching hearts would be healed when the right person came along.

Egging the house of the creator of that non-sense sounds fair, don't you think?

"I'll get changed then the shower's all yours." Darcy words snapped me from the ova poultry bombs I'd envisioned landing on an unsuspecting house as she grabbed her PJs and headed for the bathroom. I gathered my bath stuff and waited my turn. I don't think I'd ever looked more forward to a shower more than I did now.

"We need a foot massage." I blew Darcy air kisses on my way to the bathroom.

"You could sweet talk Trina at the nail salon for one of her infamous pedicures."

The record scratched and I slammed to a halt. "Excuse me?"

"She manages the nail salon on the shopping deck. Every once in a while we bribe her with treats to treat our feet."

"Did you mean for that to come out like a children's limerick?" I'm sure she did, Darcy was quite witty after all.

"You know it, babe. But seriously, I'll hook us up, but make sure to give her a nice tip in the end. You won't regret it, Vale."

When you can't remember when your last mani-pedi was that meant it had been too long. "Um, yes, please. Sign me up."

Darcy laughed as she snuggled under her blankie. "I'm so glad we're on this trip together."

"Me, too, babes. Me, too."

Chapter Two
Jack

The commotion out in the hall caught my attention and right as I opened the door, the cabin steward I'd met yesterday ran inside. One look at him and I knew something was wrong. "Hey," I called out to the group of guys converged in the hallway. "What're you up to?"

"Ahoy, Daddy!" one of them replied. His cute and innocent act was wasted on me. I'd had my fair share of manipulating boys over the years and had served my time. "Just trying to have a little fun with the cabin cutie."

That jackass needed a Daddy to paddle his arrogant ass.

"Cabin cutie is highly distraught, so I'd say his version of fun doesn't match yours. Do I need to report this incident to security?"

"Party pooper," another called out. "Fine, we'll have fun without him." The four of them walked toward the elevator, though I'd not soon forget their faces.

As soon as the elevator doors shut, so did mine. "Are you okay?" He'd taken a seat and was currently bent in half with his head between his legs, his name I'd forgotten. "Is there someone I can call for you?"

"N–no. P–please, d–don't. I'm new. I don't want to get fired."

That poor sweet boy and his nervous stutter.

"Any employer that would fire you for running from grabby hands isn't a good employer to work for. I'm sorry, your name escapes me. I'm Jack."

"Vale. We met yesterday, briefly."

Ah yes, as soon as I'd released him after nearly knocking him to the ground, he ran toward the stairwell and out of sight. "Yes, that's right. I caught you mid-fall." The scent of his bodywash was still fresh in my mind. Lilac with the slightest hint of vanilla. I'd craved sweets all night long after that.

Down, Jack. You've been on enough cruises to know the rules. Don't fraternize with the staff. The knock at the door couldn't have come at a better time before the internal debate engaged in a mental moral war.

"Can I help you?" I asked the uniformed woman who stood on the other side.

"Hello, Mr. Barrett, I'm Darcy, Vale's supervisor. He contacted me about an incident?"

"Yes, please come inside." I stepped to the side, and as soon as she entered she went directly to Vale.

"Vale, are you okay? What happened?" Darcy patted his back as she crouched down beside him.

That boy chattered so fast that I was amazed she caught any of it. Had I not witnessed the end of the altercation I'd have been completely lost.

"Mr. Barrett, you witnessed this?" Her stern gaze met mine, searching, though what for I was unsure.

"The tail end of it and I wanted to call security, but Vale was concerned for his job, so I didn't."

"Understood, but sexual harassment isn't tolerated from staff nor from guests. Are those men staying on this floor?" Her concern for Vale left me breathing a sigh of relief. She wouldn't punish him for this. She was on his side.

"Honestly, I'm not sure, but I can promise I'll keep an eye out for them." That I could guarantee.

"Vale, how many rooms do you have left to clean? I'll help you finish them."

"Oh, um, just this one."

That was interesting, he'd saved mine for last. "I'm good, I don't require any services today." I almost added I don't require daily service but a part of me was intrigued by Vale and having him in my space, even just momentarily, would allow us a bit of privacy to talk without fear of him getting into trouble.

"Thank you for your assistance, Mr. Barrett. If you need anything please don't hesitate to call us." Darcy was very formal and gave nothing away.

"Vale's not in trouble, is he?"

"No, not at all, but if you see those men, please call the steward line and ask for me."

Darcy walked ahead of Vale toward the door, when they reached it Vale whispered, "Thank you, Jack."

Though he said my name, all I heard was *Daddy.*

"You're welcome, Vale. You're safe with me." What made me add the last bit was a mystery. Vale nodded and once the door closed the room felt far too empty.

What does that mean?

It means you're losing your mind, Jack.

Well, that was a given.

I returned to the desk and the hundreds of emails that I knew my more than capable team would take care of, but constant work was in my blood. It was all I knew, though my inability to relax cost me every relationship I'd made a feeble attempt at pursuing.

Time to find a new start up to invest in, at least then my mind would be occupied until I had it off and running and move onto the next one. While it's nice to sit back and watch the companies prosper and my bank account fill, the satisfaction of a job well done wore off quicker with each endeavor.

That bone–deep ache became unbearable to ignore.

"Jesus," I cursed as I leaned back in the chair. "You're on vacation and yet here you sit, Jack. Alone by fucking choice."

Idiot.

Without another thought, mostly because I'd overthink my decision to enjoy the pool and likely not go, I slid into my swim trunks. With one of the books I'd brought in hand, off I went with a plan to hit the bar and grab a beer then settle in under the warm sun.

I'd never seen so many pride flags and signs in my life. It was as if the retail gods shipped all they'd had directly to this cruise ship. Every inch of the deck was filled with pride, literally.

Many wore flags as capes of honor with hardly anything else on.

Five minutes in line at the bar and I'd regretted having left the sanctuary of my room.

"Well, hello again, Daddy."

I scanned the familiar annoyance, though he took that as interest and not the disgust it was meant as.

"Buy me a drink, Daddy." The more he flirted the less I cared for him.

"No. I'm not contributing to any further bad behavior from you."

"Boo-hoo." His mock pout was ridiculous. "But, Daddy, I'm so cute and I always come with a happy ending. I'll even let you punish me for being naughty."

"I'll pass. A boy who thinks sexual harassment is a game isn't the boy for me."

Blink. Blink. Deer in the headlights as he scoured that pretty and very clearly empty head of his for his next words. Obviously getting turned down was rare and my doing so stunned him stupid. "We were just having a bit of fun."

"He wasn't and he was working. He could've been fired for your asinine antics."

"Oh, I didn't know that."

"It's true so make sure those so-called friends of yours know it, too, and leave Vale alone."

Past Jack would've wined and dined that hot little twink and finished the night with dessert between his cheeks. But now all I saw was a selfish, shameless imp flaunting his outer beauty to make up for the lack of inner beauty.

In a past life, had I been so blinded by orgasms I never saw beyond a sexy ass and false façade, or had I merely ignored it?

What an enlightening day this had been and it was only three pm.

He stumbled off without another word and thank fuck for that. I'd had about all of his slimy come ons I could manage. Beer in hand, I snagged what appeared to be the last available lounge chair on deck and settled in. This boat was packed which had the analytical part of my brain attempting to calculate the weight load.

Not a wise choice given there was no visible land in sight.

Read, Jack. Ignore everything around you and immerse yourself in a book just like you used to do.

And so, I did, until the combination of the pool party and the heat became too much, and I returned to my room. One freshly showered body and shaved face later I decided, what the hell, and took myself out to dinner.

"Table for one, sir?" the *maître d* asked.

"Yes, please."

Within moments of being seated, the waiter appeared. "Good evening, sir. My name is David and I'll be your waiter tonight. Would you like to start with something from the bar?"

"Yes, please. I'll have two fingers of bourbon. Neat."

"Excellent choice, sir. I'll leave you to the menu while I get your beverage."

With my palate set on surf and turf, I placed my order before he walked away and gazed out the windows at the vast ocean while I waited. Nothing but clear blue water and one of the best views of an absolutely stunning sunset. As day turned to night, the waiter appeared with my drink as if summoned by magic.

"Thank you."

"Enjoy, sir."

My gaze returned to the sea, though now it was too dark to really see. A clear view I didn't need as my mind was otherwise engaged. Here I was on a glorious vacation, alone. When this was over I'd return to my condo in Bellevue. Alone. Maybe a trip to Whidbey Island to visit my parents was in order after my return. It'd been far too long since I'd paid them a visit.

A stroll around the deck after a fabulous dinner led me to the dungeons. I'd had my fair share of leather and impact play over the years, though it wasn't where my heart lay. Having a boy was. A bit of play in the bedroom spiced things up, but the full-on leather scene wasn't what I was after. Burying my dick in tight tushes, reddened with my handprint was what I craved. Filling my boy to the brim while he came on my cock was what the best slice of heaven.

"Now, Master Patrick will demonstrate the proper use of a flogger." I wasn't familiar with the MC nor Master Patrick so I made a quick walk through the dungeon, bypassing their demonstration as I walked through the connecting rooms in the conference center. The next room was packed full of happy littles and their Daddies and Mommies, but I was most interested in viewing what they'd erected for the Pet Play area.

Wow. Color me impressed.

They had an area stanchioned off for onlookers. Behind it there was a climbing wall, which surprised me, but each pet who wished to utilize it was properly harnessed and strapped in by the staff members manning it. It appeared to be a permanent fixture and if I had to guess, this area was part of the gym which had most likely been condensed to accommodate our kinky fetishes.

In another section they'd set up a series of tunnels and mazes for the pups and one curious ferret to run through. Various kittens tumbled around the open area chasing toys and jumping at mice that dangled from the ends of sticks their handlers teased them with. Watching all of this unfold filled my heart with a sense of longing.

It was time.

Each area was separated by low, see-through dividers that served to keep the pets safe but made it possible for those who watched to have a clear view. I must admit, they did a great job with all of this. Granted, the lifestyle areas were set up and operated by the local Seattle BDSM club I was a member of, Blush, but the accommodations were more than adequate for the cruise.

One jolly pup with a case of the zoomies did laps around the tunnel area while his handler stood nearby and kept a watchful eye.

"They really did a great job, didn't they?" another voyeur addressed me. "I'm Dave."

"Jack. Nice to meet you. And yes, they did. I'm familiar with the club overseeing it out of Seattle. They run a tight show." I neglected to mention my active, yet recently unused membership and partial ownership there.

"Do you have a pet out there in the zoo?"

An untamed sigh escaped. "Sadly, no."

"Same," he replied. "I'm in the market for a new boy."

So was I, though I didn't dare curse it by saying the words aloud.

"Been playing with the little boxer running through the tubes on this trip." He smiled fondly at said pup. "Makes the cruise a bit more fun with a plus one."

"I could imagine." I was starting to feel a bit of the melancholy pain myself of being sans plus one. "Quite energetic, isn't he?"

Maybe that was the boy for me. One who was over-exuberant and full of bountiful energy. For years now I'd gone after the calm ones, ones that already had their lives in in order and didn't need a hand in organizing or even wanted a Daddy to take it over for them. My natural nurturer instincts and internalized OCD—who was I kidding, nothing about me was internalized. Shifting gears in search of a boy with similar needs as mine would be tricky, but doable.

I had faith.

I thought.

It was time to refocus on more than just sex and playtime and strive for a long-term commitment.

A partner in search of his forever.

A pet who wanted a Daddy to ease his burdens.

Did I really need to live in a condo? Wouldn't a house be better for that lifestyle? I could set up one entire room as their playroom with a miniature obstacle course and anything else they would need.

Cart-horse, Jack. You're getting wayyyy ahead of yourself.

Meh, not like I couldn't have both. Living on Whidbey, a place I loved and near my parents, was a viable option. Then keep the condo in Bellevue for anytime we go into the city. Or sell it. I wasn't in love with the place as it was.

Making plans for a life I didn't have. How pitiful was that?

The longer I stood there and watched the pets and their handlers, or Daddies, the longing became more, rendering it nearly unbearable.

Was I thinking with my head or my heart?

Where did one begin and the other end?

My thoughts were so convoluted I was incapable of sorting them.

On the way back to the room, I stopped by one of the many bars for a quick nightcap. When I walked inside my cabin, the desk lamp was on and there in the center of the perfectly made bed, not the way I left it, sat the most adorable towel origami figure in the shape of a bear.

Oh, sweet boy, you paid me a visit.

Could it be?

Or was I merely projecting?

Either way, my sights were set to learn all about that shy boy who sought solace in my room this morning. If a sense of security drew Vale from his shell, then I was just the Daddy for the job.

The remainder of the night was spent formulating a plan to learn as much as I could about Vale. With only the limited time we'd have while he cleaned my room each day, my questions had to be rapid fire and straight to the point. No lingering depth, that I'd save for later. But if I could at least get a feel for what he desired in a relationship in step one, then

I'd have a baseline in which to implement step two.

My mind whirled until near sunrise when I finally drifted off and woke with a start when I heard the keycard reader on the door beep. I bolted across the room, nearly tripped over my shoes in the process, and hurriedly shut the bathroom door.

"Mr. Barrett?" Vale called out.

"Yes, I'll be with you in a moment." I splashed my face with water, brushed my teeth and hair, then realized I had nothing but my boxers on. Well, shit. With a towel wrapped around my waist, I stepped out.

"Good morning, Vale."

"Good morning, Mr. Barrett. I'll just be a moment."

"Please, call me Jack." He blushed and turned away, though I caught a faint smile before he did. "I'm afraid I'll require an extra towel or two, please."

"Not a problem, sir."

While Vale got to work, I returned to the bathroom and dressed, reemerging a few moments later. I nearly reminded him I didn't require daily service then remembered my goal to get to know him.

"So, Vale, what do you do for fun when you're not working?" I crossed the room and sat at the desk, well out of his way.

He shrugged. "Not much. My best friend Darcy, the one you met the other day, has worked on cruise ships for a while so when she's out to sea I just hang out with my mom. Now, I'll be at sea for the next four months."

It had escaped me that crew members signed contracts for these jobs. Four months on, one month off. Not the life for me.

"Do you live in Seattle or is the port you get on at in another state?"

"Seattle, technically north of it in Lynnwood. Do you live in Seattle?"

"Belleview." *Think. Think. Think. No coffee, no clear thoughts.* "I'm ordering breakfast, would you like anything?"

"No, thank you. I already ate."

"Are you allowed to partake in any of the on-board events?" Way to dive right in, Jack. What happened to questions about him?

"Oh, um, no, sir. We're not allowed to be in the passenger areas unless it's to perform the tasks for which we were hired."

Okay, I'm batting a thousand here and sinking fast.

Not the best metaphor to use while out to sea...

"Have those guys from the other day bothered you anymore?"

"No, sir. I've only seen one of them and he went off on something about a Daddy and hands off. He lost me but he wasn't mean if that's what you're asking?"

The entire time he answered he faced away from me and I desperately wished to have his full attention.

"Vale." That did it. "If I were to have lunch here around noon tomorrow, would it be possible for you to clean my room then?"

"Oh, I don't take the dishes away. The catering team has a crew that does that."

"That's not what I meant. It was my way of asking if you'd have lunch with me."

"No fraternizing with the guests and I'm not part of the entertainment, sir." The hint of sadness in his voice was more than I could bear. Had he thought I just wanted him to pleasure me in some way?

"I didn't mean to insinuate that, nor would I use you in any way. I would like to get to know you better and just so we're clear, sex is off the table. I'm aware of the rule and wouldn't do anything to jeopardize your job. I'll understand if you decline, though I'd like to get to know the real Vale."

"I–I," he stuttered and took a moment to compose himself. "I could clean your room at noon. If you want. For tomorrow."

So adorable.

I watched as he flitted around the room. As he completed each task, he'd check it off the list on his clipboard then move onto the next. He tied the trash bags twice, fluffed a new one twice, then placed it in the bin and did the same with the pillowcases. Vale was unique in the way he completed his duties, though maybe it was because I was watching.

"I don't need the linens changed." I tried to stop him before he got too far. "How much time are you given to clean each room?"

"Twenty minutes."

Well, shit.

"What would you like to eat tomorrow then? Italian? Hamburgers? Steak? Any favorites?" *Throw me a bone here, sweet boy.*

"I'm not picky but seafood is my favorite. You really don't need to feed me. We get free food working here and it's a big menu, with all kinds of stuff. And we can eat anytime day or night," Vale rambled on.

"Understood, and I'm glad to hear that but I'd like to eat with you, and this seems the only possible way." Did that come out like a beg? Was I begging?

"True."

He mumbled to himself as he finished his work. I couldn't take my eyes off him. Every move he made, everything he touched. Mesmerized. There was no other way to put it and no way my dreams and goals wouldn't revolve around this amazing boy in front of me.

Did he know he was a boy? Had he been someone's boy or was he someone's boy?

"I should really clarify. When I asked you to lunch tomorrow, I meant as a date. You're not seeing anyone, are you?"

"No. No one dates me more than once."

"More than once?" What did I miss here?

"Yeah. I've been told I'm not dating material. Too much to handle. Talk too much. Can't sit still. You name it, they've said it." The sweet boy uttered those horrible words with resignation, and acceptance. Unacceptable in my book.

As I watched him finish his tasks, it hit me. "Are you ADHD?" It lined up with everything I saw.

"Yes. If you want to cancel tomorrow I'll totally understand."

"Cancel? Because of something that's out of your control? I'd be a sad excuse for a human if I did that." Jesus, I wasn't sure whether to celebrate this win or hunt down every jackass he'd ever dated and put the fear of God into them.

"Yeah."

"Vale, look at me." Currently he stood across the room, shifting uncomfortably from foot to foot, wringing his hands. When I saw the sadness reflected in his eyes, I crossed the room in three steps and drew him into my arms. At first, he stiffened but finally relented and relaxed into me. "I'm sorry you've only met assholes, but I can assure you, I am not one of them." He clutched the back of my shirt and nodded. "I want to get to know you, Vale, the real you. This isn't a way to pass the time on a cruise for me. I'm interested in you and I'm hoping once you return to Seattle, we can go out on a proper date in the real world."

Chapter Three
Vale

Pet Play?

Tucked away in the corner of the room, I watched as humans, not the four-legged creatures I expected to see, dressed up as cats, dogs, there was even a ferret, and they ran through the room playing with, well, pet toys.

This was not what I thought it was going to be.

Here I had snuck away from taking calls to play with the puppies and get puppy kisses.

Imagine my surprise.

But why hadn't I walked away?

Intrigued? That was the best way to describe it as I watched a silly human dressed as my favorite dog breed, a boxer, run circles around the other dogs. He barked and chased the ball his human friend threw at him. And he was happy about it.

Was this normal?

Normal was relative but still…

I wandered off, my thoughts a mixture of figuring out what the heck I'd just witnessed and worrying about lunch with Jack tomorrow. He seemed sincere but so had the others I'd attempted to date in the past. Then once they got what they wanted they were never seen nor heard from again.

Wasn't there one man out there who could handle me and my energy and want more than a piece of ass?

"There you are," Darcy announced as I walked in. "Ready to go to dinner?"

"Let's go."

"Okay, spill it," Darcy prodded as we sat with our food. "You haven't said a word since we walked in, and you're calm as fuck which isn't right."

Time to see if I was indeed insane. "On my way to meet you, after my rooms were done," I made sure to point that out, so she didn't think I was slacking. "I stopped by the pet playroom to play with the puppies."

Darcy choked on the bite she'd just taken. I hopped up, ready to give her the Heimlich but she raised her hand to stop me. "I'm okay. Just give me a minute." I waited as she took a drink, though every time she glanced at me the laughter bubbled up and over. "You thought there were real animals? Do you live under a rock? Never mind, don't answer that."

"They were people, Darcy, dressed as animals, and they were having fun."

"Sweets, I foresee you falling down a Google wormhole in the near future. Pet play is a branch of BDSM. Did you forget you were on a kink cruise?"

"That explains the scary room I passed through."

"That scary room is called a dungeon, and don't kink shame. Everyone has their outlets whether it be impact play, pet play, or littles, to name a few." Darcy got a faraway look in her eyes, and I wondered how much about my best friend I truly did not know when I thought we shared everything. "For many, BDSM isn't just about sex. It's their form of therapy, an outlet to relieve stress. And with the right partner, it's truly a beautiful thing."

"Wait, how do you know so much?"

Darcy glanced around the crowded room. "I'll explain once we're back in our room. My point being, do your research. Honestly, I think pet play would be a great outlet for all your energy. I don't know why I hadn't thought of that before."

I didn't know about that. I'd likely spend most of my time in pet time out.

So many grade school memories resurfaced...

We finished our shift and returned to our room. After I'd showered and turned out the light, Darcy finally spoke and what she said shocked the hell out of me.

"I'm a little."

"A what?" We'd been so busy after dinner I hadn't had a chance to research any of the stuff we'd talked about. I planned to do it now, but her words stopped me.

"A little. Though I don't have a Mommy of my own." Darcy's voice took on a sad, younger lilt to it. "The room next to the pet play area is for littles. If you get a chance, take a peek."

"Have you played in there?"

"No, it would be too easy to be recognized and I'd get fired. When I'm home I play at the club in Seattle as a guest of the Mommies I've met at munches. I didn't click with any of them for more than a scene or two, which is why I'm still alone. But hopefully one day I'll have a Mommy of my own."

"Understood." Though not really. I had so much to learn.

She rolled over and cuddled her blankie and said no more. I didn't want to push, it felt too personal. Instead, I pulled the covers over my head and dove into the wormhole Darcy warned of.

Who knew any of this even existed?

Pet play is a dynamic within the BDSM community and involves an individual participating in a Dominant/submissive relationship portraying an animal and while doing so, being treated as such. This generally includes dressing as that pet and acting out how to react within their pack. An example of this is one dressed as a puppy, walking or running around on all four legs, barking, chasing a ball and receiving accolades and treats from their handler for being a good pet.

For some, they even go so far as to nap in a pet bed while in gear. Pet play can be sexual or non-sexual, given whatever was agreed upon prior to engaging in a scene by all parties involved. That is of the utmost importance before any pet is allowed to enter into subspace. Trust is everything within this dynamic.

This is generally a Dom/sub activity and much like within the BDSM realm, pet play does involve collaring as the partners progress within their relationship. Some animals will wear a leash while others opt out of using such a restraint.

As with any relationship, pet play is what you and your partners make of it, but we encourage all parties involved to set limits beforehand, establish safe words, and sign an explicitly detailed contract that breaks down what acts you are and are not willing to engage in. Remember, no means no.

Pet play, as with any engagement in the BDSM community, is a beautiful, therapeutic means to releasing energy and receiving gratification, whether it be sexual or otherwise.

From there it was a series of videos, none of which scared me but all of which intrigued me. Could pet play be the outlet I'd waited my entire life for? One where I wasn't the token weirdo who couldn't control himself. I know fitting in isn't all it's cracked up to be but it sure would be nice to have like-minded friends and not be the oddball anymore.

Not to mention there was a certain anonymity that came along with wearing a costume, such as not losing my job. But where would I find an animal outfit and on such short notice?

As soon as the alarm on Darcy's phone went off, I hopped up and whistled a cheery tune as I made the bed.

"I don't know how you do it." Darcy stretched and shut off the alarm. "When I get less than even six hours of sleep I'm a grouch, yet you survive on four and are always so freaking cheerful."

I danced around and gathered my work outfit, feeling much like Cinderella only there were no birds flitting around, gathering pieces for my ball gown.

"Okay, even for you this is too much. Spill it." Darcy's demand went ignored until the pillow she launched hit my head.

"What? Can't I be in a good mood?" Jeez, non-morning people were so grouchy.

"Not this annoyingly good. Now, what gives?"

The immovable stance she took up blocked the path between our beds and didn't leave me with much choice.

"Promise you won't get mad first."

Likely not the best choice of words given her growl.

"Now, butthead."

"That's not nice, but fine. I have a lunch date. At least, I think it's a date? Yeah, yes, he said it was a date."

"You have a date? With whom?"

She may be some future Mommy's little but right now she claimed the role of my keeper. "Um, Jack."

"Jack, Jack, Jack," she repeated, trying to picture who the name went with. "I don't know any Jack on staff that you've met."

"He's, um, not staff."

Oh, that look was not a happy one. "No! No! No! No! Hell to the mother fucking no, Vale."

"It's in his room while I clean. He ordered lunch. It's a working lunch date. No one will see us, I swear." Fuck! Fuck! Fuck!

"I put my neck on the line for you and I even got them to approve our sharing a room. If you get caught, we both get canned." Cue in the guilt trip. For someone who wasn't a mom, she sure had the way of the mother down.

"I won't, I promise."

Darcy stormed off and had the doors had the ability to slam, the bathroom one would've just done so. Not wanting to further piss her off, I made sure all I had left to do when she came out was brush my teeth and hair, so I was ready to roll when she was.

We walked to the dining hall, during which she said nothing.

We got our food and took a seat, still nothing.

We got to our supply rooms—zip, zilch, nada.

I grabbed my cart and headed to my rooms and contemplated canceling lunch, though I really didn't want to. But by the time I got to Jack's room, I was prepared to do so until I stepped foot inside.

"Wow." The curtains were wide open, and sunshine filled the room. He had the dining table pulled to the center with a white tablecloth draped across it. Atop it sat a pair of candle holders, sticks lit and two plates with silver domes covering them.

"Hello, Vale. Please, take a seat."

Too stunned to disobey and now far too excited to cancel, I sat as Gentleman Jack pulled the chair out for me.

"It smells wonderful."

Jack uncovered my dish before doing his. "Surf and turf, no pun intended, but it's one of my favorite meals. I hope you enjoy it."

Wiggling as I ate, a mixture of yummy excitement and my inability to sit for long periods of time was the norm but sadly it didn't go unnoticed.

"You okay over there?" Jack asked, no anger to his words, but still I froze.

"Yes, sorry."

"No need to apologize. It's adorable." His watchful gaze was glued to me, which only increased the squirms.

Adorable? No one had ever called him that before. *Sit still. What's wrong with you? I'll make your ass hurt so you have a reason to squirm.* Yeah, I left mid dinner during that date. But if Jack noticed my discomfort, he chose not to comment on it.

"So, Vale, why don't you tell me about yourself."

Blank. It was like someone just took a giant eraser and scrubbed my brain.

"Vale?"

I got up and paced the cabin. Jack let it go on for a couple of rounds before addressing it.

"Did I say something wrong, Vale?"

"You're nice to me and didn't yell about my squirming. You asked me questions and I forgot my name. Are you for real?" Was he being paid to play with me? Was Darcy keeping that secret and maybe she was mad at herself and not at me? Did my mom pay him to be nice to me? Shit, did I say that last part out loud?

"No one is paying me to be nice to you, Vale."

Yup, I did.

Well, shit.

"I don't believe I know anyone who knows you outside of Darcy and I only met her the one time when she came to get you. Based upon your comments, I venture to guess you haven't dated the nicest of men."

"The word *date* is stretching it. Most didn't go past a single date. One time I left because he threated to spank me if I didn't sit still. I don't like to be spanked so if you do this needs to end now." That was something I wouldn't budge on. My own mother never spanked me and in my eyes no one but her had that right to. I get it, it was some people's kink and that's fine, but it's not mine.

Jack smiled and crossed the room toward me. "Sweet boy, spankings are only given to those who are accepting of them, whether it be for play or punishment. Knowing that's a hard limit for you..." My brain scrambled in search of those words I knew I read last night. "Spanking is off the table so please, don't worry that handsome head of yours. Come, sit down and finish your lunch while we talk."

As soon as I sat, the floodgates opened. "I'm bad at dating. Hyperactive. Guys don't like that. They don't like me. It's ADHD now. Sometimes I can control it but not always. I'm not a virgin, but I haven't had a lot of experience. Oh my god, did I just word vomit all of that?"

At this point, Jack had a hard time holding back his laughter and when it burst forth I couldn't help but smile. "I'm sorry, Vale. I'm not laughing at you, really I'm not. But that was the most you've said to me in all our encounters, and it was a lot of information at one time." He gestured to my plate for me to finish while he drank most of his water. "All right, let's tackle each item. One, you've dated assholes and on behalf of gay men everywhere, I apologize for that. The fact they mistook your neurodiversity for naughtiness makes me want to hunt them down and give them a stern talking to."

Neurodiverse.

None of the men I dated used that word. Oh, they used several others, none of which were nice, but they were clearly uneducated on my lifelong challenge.

"There are many outlets and exercises you can engage in to help channel your energy. Had they been worthy of you, they would've made suggestions to that." Jack shook his head, clearly bothered by this.

"Why did that guy in the hallway the other day call you Daddy?"

It was like once I started, I couldn't stop and out came every question and thought.

"Well, he was being a smart ass but ironically, I am a Daddy who is also a handler. Do you know what that means?"

"Only what I read last night."

"I take it being exposed to kink on this cruise is new to you?"

My head bobbed up and down. "Yes, though I read some about it last night after I saw the scary room and Darcy told me she was a little." I slapped my hand over my mouth. "Oh my god. She'll kill me if she ever finds out I said that. Please don't tell her."

"I promise, your secret is safe with me. Let's touch on the scary room comment. What part of that room scared you?"

"There was a guy tied to this cross thingy and another guy was hitting him with something like a whip with tentacles. I don't like pain and I'd freak out if I was tied up. Do you like those things?" *Please say no, please say no.*

Jack sighed. "In a past life, I did engage in impact play, though it's not a make it or break item in a relationship for me. I'm a Daddy. A natural caregiver. I've had littles and while they're fun, my interests lie more in pet play. Did you go into that room?"

"Did you play with that guy? Is that why he called you Daddy?"

"No. I've never played with him nor will I. He's more of a brat and I prefer good boys." Jack paused and I wasn't sure if I should say more or wait. "Pet play is a great way to get out of your head and gain exercise at the same time."

Get out of my head, oh how I hoped that would happen for me. The damn thing ran a million miles a minute and the fucking squirrels were always in charge.

"Well, if you get a chance, pop into the pet playroom and look around. Maybe do an online search or feel free to ask me any questions you may have." Was this guy for real? Lunch, nice comments, come to him with questions? There had to be a fault somewhere.

Did I tell him I already had, or keep it to myself until I figured it out? I landed on keeping my mouth shut and a simple nod and shoveled more food in. Full mouth = inability to speak. Jack too returned to eating as we sat in silence and finished our meals. I knew my mind was a swirly mess of questions and likely his was, too, but it was good to hear he hadn't messed around with that dillhole who tried to lure me into his room.

Not that I had any say in what Jack did or who he did it with.

Nor should I.

All the praying to the gayest of gay deities wouldn't land me a man as handsome as Jack.

At least not for more than an orgasm...

Chapter Four
Jack

Vale's leg bounced underneath the table. I wondered if he was aware of that. Was it nerves? The ADHD? Or a combination of both? While I knew bits and pieces about that particular disorder I wasn't well versed, though I soon would be.

"Are you expecting sex? That's off the table for me. Not until I get to know a person well. Not that anyone wants to get to know me. The few times I've had it wasn't good, or meaningful. Sex is supposed to mean something, at least to me." The sweet boy sighed. "They just left without taking care of me."

I didn't know whether to rush off and defend his honor or silently cheer for the chance to prove to him how beautiful sex could be. But the time didn't feel right to address that.

"As I mentioned yesterday, sex is off the table for now. Did you get enough to eat?" The Daddy in me wouldn't be ignored and he'd already latched onto Vale in a ridiculously quick time.

"Yes, thank you." Vale wiped his mouth, folded his napkin, unfolded it, then folded it again.

"Something on your mind, Vale?"

"Well, um, yes. How old are you? What do you do for a job? Do you have a boyfriend?" My face widened in a smile at his rapid-fire questions.

"Okay, in order. I'm thirty-eight. I invest in startup companies and I'm single. Your turn."

His shy grin was adorable. "I'm twenty-two, I believe you know what I do, and I likely covered my dating status earlier with the whole lack of filter thing."

"You, dear Vale, are a delightful breath of fresh air." Another sweet grin as he wiggled in his seat. "Any more questions?

"Sooo many, but I have to go. Breaktime is over. What do you need cleaned before I leave?" He glanced around the tidy room. I'd taken care of that prior to our lunch date. Selfish, yes, I wanted all of his time focused on me and not on cleaning.

"Absolutely nothing. Can we do this again? Say same time tomorrow?"

"Okay, yes." Vale readily agreed.

"Great, then it's a date."

"Date? This was a d-date? And you want another one?"

His beautiful light brown, almost amber eyes implored mine as he sought the truth in my words. That poor, mistreated boy. "Yes, Vale. I wish for many more dates with you."

"Eeep!" burst forth quicker than the hand he slapped over his mouth to block it did. "Sorry. But I have to ask, are you sure?"

"Very sure."

"But this is all I can do. We can't like, really go out-go out. Just hidden lunches like dirty secrets. Which we're not. I didn't mean it that way."

"I didn't take it that way. When do you get back to port?"

"Not soon enough."

I'd never held such a position, one aboard a cruise ship, therefore I wasn't versed in the behind-the-scenes part, though I now wondered what happened if it didn't work out with an employee. Did they stick them on a raft and radio the coast guard their location? Lock them up somewhere? Hmm, inquiring minds and all that, and this one needed to know.

"Well, we can tackle that beast when the time comes. In the interim, I'd like to have as much of your time as you are willing and able to give me." Too forward? Too fast? Appears reining myself in wasn't an option no matter the setting.

"Okay. Yes." Vale again answered with a resounding head bob, which I'd come to learn went hand in hand with a yes reply. "But I really have to go." Vale hopped up, kissed my cheek and was out the door before what he'd done had registered.

That lunch date went well. I think...

I spent the rest of the afternoon researching hyperactivity related ADHD and absorbed as much as possible. My mind whirled with ideas to assist Vale even though it kept falling back on pet play. He'd look so adorable as a pup or even a kitten, nudging toys and doing laps around the ring. Hopefully he'd take my advice and peek into the playroom.

The remainder of the afternoon I waffled back and forth between work emails and surfing the pet play sites. It had been forever since I'd been on them, having played with boys who had already established their pets and such. Now this time I searched with Vale in mind, the boy I wanted to be mine.

What kind of boy would I see him as?

What was the ideal pet for him?

I had played the role of a handler who was also a Daddy and I envisioned Vale as my pup. A kitten would be cute and coy, but I saw him as something more. Something more energetic, like a boxer. Or even a monkey. Lord, that boy would make a cute monkey. Jumping off faux trees in the play area. Probably not a good idea, unless they were firmly secured in place, and he was strapped into harnesses to catch his fall. But I bet you anything once we are both ashore we'll find his fit. He might enjoy date nights that included activities such as zip-lining or various kinds of obstacle courses. What a great way for us both to get exercise and enjoy cozy naps together afterward.

The wheels rapidly turned as Vale became another obsession of mine, as all of my business dealings had been. But I'd do well to remember this was a human and not a business and keep the human aspect to the forefront, though the drive to excel as his partner would be no less.

How sad was it that anything I did was compared to a business transaction?

Two days of getting to know Vale and already I was a million miles ahead in the vast world of dating.

Who are you and what have you done with the confirmed bachelor, Jack Barrett?

I stood and stretched and glanced out the balcony door, catching the last glimpse of sunset. My ass was numb, and my hand cramped from jotting down the notes I'd taken as the ideas came non-stop, and I couldn't wait to share these future plans with Vale. But it was time to get out of this room.

The party was hopping as I took a quick walk along the outside deck through the throngs of, well, barely there thongs. Speedos had more to them than the splashes of material these guys had on. When an all too familiar, "Ahoy, Daddy," rang out from a nearby group—*great, now he's got his merry band of idiots joining in*—I speed-walked back inside and straight into the dining area.

After the heavy lunch with Vale, I opted for a chicken Caesar salad to keep it light then spent the remainder of the evening doing a bit of gambling in the casino. It'd been forever since I played blackjack. With a fresh drink in hand, I sidled up to the table and made a wager.

I had no idea why I continued to glance at my phone. The likelihood there was reception in the casino was minimal, nor had I remembered to give Vale my number. Something I'd remedy tomorrow during our next lunch date.

As I placed a bet, my mind wandered back to his sweet smile, and the way he blushed at compliments. Every word was heartfelt from what I'd captured about Vale in the short time we'd known one another. A boy in need of being shown what love and kindness was from a worthy partner solely focused on him and not themselves. With each passing moment, the desperation to be that man intensified. To be the man who claimed their place in his heart and soul.

My focus was shit and even though I was ahead, it was time to call it a night. I took the long way back to my cabin through the common area where the shops and dining were. I loved how they had the open area in the center with trees and plants to make you feel like you were dining outdoors. Beautiful twinkle lights adorned the trees and created a romantic atmosphere. Vendors were hopping, working their way through the extensive lines of patrons they had. This was without a doubt a sold-out cruise.

Of course, in the end, I ended up in the pet room again. The happy animals and their handlers brought me happiness, though the longing intensified with each visit. I hoped to someday be out there. Not necessarily on this cruise but at the Blush, hopefully showing off my new pet.

The little boxer from the night before and his handler who'd spoken with me weren't here. The little ferret was and a couple of new kittens along with an animal I couldn't quite make out. Which was irrelevant. He was having a good time and that's what this was all about. I watched them frolic and play for a while, then wandered next door to the littles' room. But it just didn't hit me like the pets did. When all was said and done, I decided to call it a night.

As I lay in bed, the balcony curtains open and stared out into the moonlight night, I longed for Vale to be here beside me. Flesh on flesh, as I took my time getting acquainted with his body, memorizing every spot that elicited sexy sounds from the boy. To bring him to the edge, time and again before finally allowing him to topple over. He'd come so hard he'd pass out. I'd clean his lithe body and watch as he napped, awaiting his next arousal when we'd begin again.

A man could dream, couldn't he?

Too restless to sleep, and now horny as hell. What else was a man to do but take his own cock in hand and bring about his own pleasure? Envisioning those honey eyes staring up at me, his lips wrapped around my shaft. Up and down his mouth would slide, tongue circling the underside of the crown just the way I liked it. Stray drool escaping between his lips and dribbling down onto my balls.

Fucking hell, that was the hottest thing I've ever imagined.

I stroked harder, faster. The only sounds in the room were my furious hand ministrations and breathless pants. Each time I pictured Vale's debauched face, my balls crept up and tightened uncomfortably.

When he moaned around my shaft, it was as though he was actually there, between my legs, and that sent me careening over the edge.

"Fuck." The release hit me in a furious rush and dream Vale consumed every last drop.

How would I be able to look Vale in the eye tomorrow and not picture his swollen lips and that dream face staring up at me?

My cock made a valiant attempt at recovery but in the end, failed. Second and even the rare third round were harder to obtain at my age. I cleaned myself off, cuddled the extra pillow and fell asleep to pleasant thoughts of the sweet boy I wished were here.

I heard his cart before I saw him as I peeked around the door. *Nosey much*, I thought to myself, as I tried to guesstimate how much longer it would be before Vale got here. A quick glance in the hallway showed there were about two or three more rooms between us from where his cart stood. I'd already ordered lunch, which would be here soon. The selfish side of me wanted more time with him today, so I didn't tidy up as I had yesterday. I wouldn't have him do all the cleaning himself because that wasn't fair but at least we could still talk while I helped him straighten up.

I hopped in the shower and right as I stepped out, a knock at the door came. I hoped it was catering and not Vale. Thankfully, when I answered it, it was so while the staff set up the table for lunch I hurried and got ready because I knew Vale wasn't far behind them. A few minutes after they left, he appeared.

"Good afternoon, Vale. Come on in." He walked inside and glanced around. The tension in his shoulders said it all, he wasn't happy with the state of the room. "There's a method to this madness, I swear."

"It's not your job to clean your room, Jack, it's mine. I'll get to work."

"It was my hope that we could do it together after lunch. It would give us a bit more time to talk. Shall we eat first?" He nodded and sat in the chair I pulled out. One thing my mother would never allow was for me to not act like a gentleman. She raised me better than that.

"Ooohhh, lasagna. Chef makes the best lasagna."

"Glad you like it. So how has your day been so far?" These weren't scripted questions, I truly cared to hear how his day went.

"Not too bad, but it's pretty much the same routine every day. I think we've got two more days at sea before we dock at the first island, but I'm not positive. I've kind of lost track of time since it's rare that I get above deck and see the sunlight."

"That doesn't sound like much fun." I wished I could take him out for a walk in the fresh air. Take in a sunset together, unwind with a night out.

"No, it's not. But at least it's a job, and hopefully I can keep this one for the duration of my contract."

"Understood. So how was your evening last night?" A change of subject was in order before the dear boy berated himself over lost jobs.

"We worked until ten. By the time we got back to our room, I showered and did some more research on stuff."

I had an inkling that stuff equaled pet play given yesterday's conversation.

"Darcy and I started cleaning out the storage rooms down below. So we're slowly working our way through those while the rest of the team runs the guest calls."

"I can't imagine how long some of that stuff must have been down there. Lost to the catacombs of the ship." I'm sure most nonperishables were stored below deck and at times forgotten. Who knew the age of those items.

"Let's just say I had to put on a mask because there was so much dust." Vale shuddered. "My allergies were out of control."

"That doesn't sound like fun."

"No, it wasn't but the OCD part of my brain does enjoy organizing and setting things right. Plus, it passes the time and wears me out so I can get a couple more hours of sleep than I'm used to. Honestly, Darcy was right about this job. It has helped with that, though I still have never slept a full night."

"Never as in never?" Even given the research I'd done I hadn't come across that side note related to it.

"Never as in never, Jack."

"Have you given anymore thought to pet play? I did some research on ADHD and neurodiversity and I believe it would be a great outlet for you." He paused mid bite and I feared I'd said the wrong thing.

"You–you did that for me?"

"Of course, I did. I mean, I'm kind of hoping this is more than just a cruise fling for you and given what you said yesterday, it doesn't sound like that's the way you operate. I know you don't know me well, but that's not how I work either." Had I misunderstood? I sure as hell hoped not.

The tension he'd been carrying in his shoulders relented and they dropped. "You don't know how happy I am to hear that. I was so afraid that I was nothing more than someone to pass the time with while you were on the ship. I mean, I know you leave the room because I've come by before and cleaned when you weren't here. Well, that one time. But still..."

"I think I know where this is going so let me set the record straight. As already discussed, I'm not seeing anybody else. Not that we're really seeing each other, but I like to think that we are, if that makes any sense." When he nodded, I knew I hadn't lost him and continued. "When I go out at night, it's alone. When I come back to my room, it's alone. And I don't go to anybody else's room either because the only person I want to spend any time with on this ship and even once this cruise is over is the very person sitting across from me right now." That cute blush reappeared. I reached across the table and placed my hand over his. "Vale, I'd like to see where this goes when you're back on solid ground. If that sounds like something you'd like to do, that is."

"Yes, please and thank you."

"Such a sweet, polite boy."

"I try and my mom wouldn't like it if I acted any other way."

"Well, that's the perfect segue into our next conversation. Tell me about your family."

"Not much to tell. It's always just been me and my mom. No brothers or sisters. Well, kind of my pseudo sister, Darcy, who you've met. My mom adores her. Other than that, there's no one else. Well, cousins here and there but we don't see them much. What about you?" I loved the way his thoughts came out, completely unfiltered. No time to cover anything up, just the plain, simple truth. So rare to find in this day and age.

"Similar story, although my parents are still together, and they live on Whidbey Island. I actually plan to go there for a couple of weeks once the ship docks back in Seattle. I'm a workaholic, though I'm working on that. No pun intended." Vale smiled. "I'm learning to let go and enjoy life while I'm still young enough to do that. I've worked for as long as I can remember. Basically, doing the same thing my father has done and he was able to retire young. I've always admired him and enjoyed going on adventures as I called them when he'd take me on business trips. It was a no brainer I'd follow in his footsteps after college. Thankfully, he had many lucrative deals already in place when I stepped in and from time to time when I need him, he's there for me to pick his brain. For the most part, all of our investments operate like well-oiled machinery."

"Wow, that's awesome. And you're still so young. I mean, in your thirties and you're only halfway to retirement age and now you could technically retire."

Most dates, boys, whatever you wanted to call past conquests, when they learned what I did I could see the literal dollar signs in their eyes. But not with Vale. Awe, interest, excitement—those were some of what I saw in his.

"I could, but retiring without a partner just doesn't sound like much fun to me."

"True, but you could travel like you're doing now and see the world." Vale got a faraway look in his eyes as if envisioning places on his bucket list.

"Truth be told, my assistant and my chief of staff booked this trip for me and kinda shoved me onto the boat. That was their not-so-subtle way of telling me to take a vacation and get out of their hair." Diana, my assistant, had to have been the mastermind or it never would've been executed.

Vale giggled. "I don't even know them, and I already like them. So, tell me about all the places you've been and where else you want to go."

He held on to my every word, enthralled with the stories and the life I've lived as he absorbed every bit of it. I'd never garnered such attention from someone who didn't earn a paycheck from me, and it was a welcome change.

"I'm not sure we have enough time for that, and I don't want to get you into trouble, so I'll just hit the highlight reel. I've been to every continent, but not every country. I've never taken a date with me to any of them. Every trip I've been on has been business related, even though at times I did take a couple extra days and did a bit of sightseeing. So long story short, I've never gone on a destination vacation outside of this one that wasn't work related. I find little to no appeal to visit places alone, but I think the idea behind this trip was that I would find someone, if only for the duration of the cruise and that was better than nothing to them. Little did they know that I would find someone that I still wished to see once I got home."

Chapter Five
Vale

"Hold on, Darcy." That girl was insanely driven when she had a goal in mind. And for some reason, she was hell bent on cleaning out these rooms. But even with the mask, the coughing fits came thanks to all the dust that filled the air. I sat back on a big box and sank inside. "Oof!"

"Oh my God, Vale, are you okay?" She wiggled her way through the sea of boxes to help me out and it took more than one pull to get me loose from the giant box I was stuck in.

"What is this big brown thing?" I tugged at the bundle of matted fur and couldn't make heads or tails of it, so I pulled it out of the box. "It's a giant costume of what I think was once a monkey, maybe a gorilla or a deranged bear." The thing was gangly and quite frightening.

She laughed when I put the mask on. It was a vintage headpiece that weighed at ton. "That thing is awful, and I don't think anybody's gonna want to wear it. I'd put it in the trash pile, it's falling apart. We can offload it with the rest of this stuff when we get back to Seattle."

But the wheels were already turning. "I think I could make something of it. Thanks to my mother's insistence, I learned how to sew. Is there a sewing machine around here?"

"I think there's a couple of them. I know there's a tailor on board. He might have some if none of the ones we have work. Hold on a sec." Darcy wandered down the hall and came back a few minutes later with one. "Here, try this. I don't know how to use them. What are you planning to do with that monstrosity?"

"If we're just going to throw this costume away, I'm wondering if I might be able to have it?"

"What's going on in that zippy little head of yours, Vale?"

"Well, if I tell you, are you going to get mad at me like you did when I had lunch with Jack?" I hadn't shared that it had become a daily thing, no need to set her off again.

"I'm still not happy about that, but no one's said anything and as long as it stays that way we're good. So back to this," she gestured to the giant head I held, "what's the plan here?"

"I've been doing a lot of research on pet play, and I was kind of hoping to check out that room, but I need a costume that covers me, so I don't get caught. I'm just hoping to finally find an outlet for all this energy."

"Vale," she got that sympathetic yet scolding mother sound in her voice. "You better make sure every inch of your handsome face is covered."

I flirtingly batted my lashes. "You think I'm handsome?"

"Handsome in the annoying *little brother's going to end up getting us both in trouble* way. Just please, promise you'll be careful, Vale."

"I promise, Mother."

"Smart ass."

We worked as long as our bodies could before we called it a day. I tucked the costume away in a corner, out of the line of sight. If I hauled it up to our room, there'd be no space for either of us. My thought process with this monstrosity was to work down here cutting away and saving what material I could and then take the pieces along with the sewing machine up to our room and get to work on a new costume. That way, the box of discarded pieces was down here to get hauled away with the rest of the trash.

"I still think you're crazy," Darcy said, "but I respect and understand your need for an outlet, a way to find and center yourself." She gazed off and I knew where her thoughts had wandered since she'd opened up and shared that personal aspect of herself with me.

"I wish we would have known these things about ourselves sooner. Well, I mean, I guess you did, but you hadn't told me. I do understand the need to keep some things to yourself. But still..." The words trailed off. A tinge of hurt was still there, though I was working past it. This was her story, not mine and she wasn't obligated to tell me everything.

"I didn't keep that from you to hurt you. But in the beginning, I didn't understand the little part of myself until I researched it. Just as you're doing now with pet play. I mean, yes, at times the internet is a breeding ground for idiots, but there are some good sites which you've obviously landed on because you've learned a lot. I mean, look at you now, you're making your own costume to put yourself out there and give it a try. I think that's fantastic and brave. Trust me, there's nothing else I'm keeping from you and if I ever find a Mommy, you'll be the first to know."

We showered and went to bed, but my mind just wouldn't stop so I snuck out of the room and back down to the storage area with a pair of scissors in hand and immediately got to work cutting out the usable pieces of material and setting them aside.

I had an idea of how I wanted this to look, though ideas and reality didn't always align and having it turn out like some cheap ass mascot with patches of fur pasted everywhere wasn't gonna fly. Diligence in covering private and recognizable areas was the main focus.

Creating a pair of shorts and a top, or possibly making it all one piece if I could save the zipper from the current costume, would be tricky. I got to work, trimming the fur down so it wasn't as long and bushy. Even in my mind that didn't sound right.

I was going for more of a monkey than a gorilla or an ape, which this was and by the looks of it, circa 1970. The giant head was cheesy and heavy and unbearable for my use. I drew up a design for a mask of sorts that covered my face with cute ears. The lighter colored chest pieces would work for the center of the ears. The original costume didn't have a tail, so I'd make one and attach it to the shorts. Basically, this was an act of desperation, but I was determined to make it work.

As long as the pieces didn't fall off and skin was revealed, I'd be okay.

I think...

By three a.m., my eyes were floaty, and my body had had enough. I slipped inside our cabin and showered again given I was covered in dust and old gross pieces of what was once go–rilla fur. Hopefully when all was done I could hand wash it and get rid of the stale stench. Who wanted to play with a stinky monkey?

"You're not as sly as you think you are, Vale," Darcy mentioned over breakfast the next morning. "I heard you slip out and back in."

"I'm sorry, I didn't mean to wake you up, but I couldn't sleep. All these ideas for the costume wouldn't wait, so I thought I'd get started on it." If I wore my mind out, I was able to sleep even if only for a few hours.

"I get it, I know how that mind of yours never stops, especially once you've got an idea in it, such as making a costume."

She wasn't wrong. Everything with me be–came an obsession, whether I wanted it to or not. My mind was complex, and constantly spun until it figured out everything between A and Z. It would exhaust every potential out-come before it would accept failure. This time, failure wasn't an option, but it would accept a temporary fix until something permanent could be obtained. Even when I mostly focused on one thing, there were still several other squirrels on the mental treadmill at the same time inside that crazy skull of mine.

"As soon as you're done with your cabins, radio me and I'll meet you in the storage room. I want to see if we can get finished tonight. I'm ready to be done with that project. Speaking of which, how far did you get on yours?"

I followed Darcy to dump our trash and re-turn the trays as we exited the dining hall.

"Not much. I spent the time cutting out the areas of material that I could reuse and stuffed the rest of it, along with that ginormous head, back into the box to go to the dump. I'll take those pieces and a sewing machine up to our room, and then I can help you finish the stor-age room."

"These tasks have definitely made for some long nights, and my brain needs a break. So let's try to get out of there by eight p.m. if we can."

"That would be great, then I can work on the costume some more. Would be nice to get that done so I could test it out." Fingers crossed my design and execution meshed. "Do you know what hours the playrooms are open?"

"I don't think there are set times because the cruise has events going on twenty-four-seven, much like Vegas. There are different crew and club members on shift in each room so that the rooms and patrons are protected the entire time."

That made total sense. I'd hate to hear somebody got hurt playing while open let alone when it wasn't. Well, the probability that it would be me was very high. Especially since I didn't have a handler. Could I ask Jack? Maybe it would be best to wait and see how this suit turned out before I risked embarrassing myself in front of him.

Ugh, I foresaw a nasty face plant in my clumsy ass future...

"You look exhausted," Jack said as I stepped inside his room.

"Aren't you a sweet talker." Ugh, how quickly things had turned.

"Sweet boy, I meant no disrespect but it's in my nature to worry. You are absolutely, without a doubt the most adorable man I've ever met but one who clearly is not getting enough rest." He reached out to me but hesitated. "I'm sorry, I must value personal boundaries. May I have a hug?"

I dove into his arms, headfirst into his chest and nearly knocked the wind from him. "Oof!" Jack stepped back as he wrapped his arms around me. "I take it I wasn't the only one eagerly awaiting a hug." I nodded, and even though he couldn't see it, he felt it. "This is wonderful, but before we get too far into our lunch date, I want to make sure we exchange phone numbers and email addresses. So as time allows, we can still contact each other. I know reception on the ship is terrible but at least we do have internet service to email, and it won't cost either of us a small fortune."

"Yes, I agree." I handed Jack my phone and he immediately entered his info, and his phone dinged a couple seconds later.

"I texted myself, so I have your number as well, but make sure and text me your email address." I furiously typed it and his phone dinged a second time. "Thank you, sweet boy. Now, let's eat."

"Your room is clean again. You don't want me to stay longer.?" Had our lunches become cumbersome and boring? Was he done with me already?

"Oh, I do. But instead of putting us both to work again like I did yesterday—by the way, sorry about that. I should've have thought that idea out more beforehand. Today I figured the extra time together could be spent chatting. I really enjoy our lunchtime talks and getting to know you better."

"Ditto. It's a nice break in my mundane days. Otherwise, all I do is clean, clean, clean."

"Is that what's kept you up at night?"

"For the most part, like I'd mentioned, I'm not much of a sleeper. Generally, I get four or five hours a night. But we've been cleaning the storage rooms which is filthy and exhausting, though we're hoping to get done tonight at a decent time. Darcy and I are wiped out." An answer without an answer. It felt wrong not telling the whole truth, but I wasn't ready to give that secret away.

"The Daddy in me wants to be stern and set a bedtime for you, but I know we're not there yet. Plus, based upon what you've told me already, it's likely a waste of time. You know your limits and you know when you reach them. But maybe together we can find a way to help you sleep better."

I wanted to tell him about the costume and that I was gonna try the pet play as he had suggested, but I didn't want to get too far ahead of myself, in case the whole thing went to shit when I began sewing it together.

"I see those wheels turning and when you're ready to share, I'm here to listen."

"Thank you." I loved that he wasn't pushy like some guys who would've pushed. Sadly, before long our lunch was over, and I had to say goodbye.

Jack rose and extended a hand to help me up. Ever the gentleman. "Would it be too forward of me to ask for a kiss?"

Even if I wanted to say no, which I didn't, my head wouldn't have it as it all too eagerly bobbed up and down.

With one arm around my waist, Jack pulled me against him. His fingers traced along my cheekbone and across my lips. Even though it had only been days that we'd known one another, it felt like I'd waited for this forever. He pressed his lips to mine in the gentlest of touches. Sweet, but I hoped for more. Soon, one kiss led to another and when Jack's tongue trailed along the seam of my lips, my mouth parted and his tongue slid inside.

Mine eagerly met his in what I hoped was the first of many dances. I loved kissing and missed it terribly having not dated in so long. Though some from my past whatever you want to call them never gave me more than a simple peck, and to me a kiss spoke volumes. It could be sweet and gentle as ours had started out, timid in the beginning, then escalated to defcon five. A prelude to something more, a happy ending. Or just a way to really get to know a love interest. With Jack my entire body tingled, and my cock hardened. These work slacks were unforgiving and there was no way to hide an erection in them.

"Now that was a solid kiss," Jack said as we drew back, and he kissed the tip of my nose. "I look forward to tomorrow's lunch date."

"Me, too. Have a good day and feel free to text me or email me, but know that it'll be a while before I can respond sometimes. But as soon as I can, I will." Nervous much, Vale? That kiss scrambled my brain.

"I understand." Jack winked and the silly gesture did nothing to deflate my cock. "Until tomorrow."

"Until tomorrow."

By the time Darcy and I finished the room, it was nearly ten. So much for our eight o'clock goal and my endless energy had topped out. Cleaning the rooms and reorganizing the storage area drained me. Had I attempted to venture to the play area tonight I wouldn't have had the energy to do more than watch. After I'd showered I dozed off, though two hours later I was wide awake, quietly hand-sewing the pieces I had measured and cut to put together. I didn't dare use the machine, it would have woken Darcy up and all hell would break loose. I'd just run up tomorrow after my cabins were done to finish up and then try it on.

Fingers crossed all went well.

Chapter Six
Jack

"I'm sorry, Monkey. Every pet must have a handler or a Daddy to escort them into the play area. No unattended playmates." I walked into one of the staff addressing a new...

Wait a second.

"Sorry, I'm late, Little Monkey." Calling Vale by name wouldn't do. Not only would it risk his job, but it wasn't a suitable pet name. Not that Little Monkey was, though it did fit him to a tee.

"Do you two know each other?" the attendant asked Vale and he nodded. Taking that response to be acceptable, the attendant moved on.

"Working late cleaning storage rooms, huh?" I whispered once the guy was out of earshot.

"We were but then afterward I worked on the suit. I found it in a box in one of the rooms we cleaned out. It was going into the trash pile when it hit me to make a costume from it. Be honest, how bad is it?" I glanced down at the ensemble he'd prepared. I had no idea what he'd used for the pieces. It reminded me of a raggedy old bear I'd had as a child paired with a bathroom rug, but I wasn't going to embarrass him by saying that. He'd obviously worked very hard on it.

"It'll do, Cheeky Monkey, and it covers the important parts. Now, is there another name you'd like to go by while here? Or what would you like me to call you?" Pet names were important. Some named themselves after pets they'd once had while others merely winged it.

"I like Little Monkey."

"Little Monkey it is then. Now, where would you like to start? Climb the wall, or the obstacle course, or do you want to swing along the over-sized cat towers?" Hopefully they were secured in place to handle human weight. Vale glanced around the area, mentally calculating his plan of attack. Every space except for the climbing wall was occupied.

"Can I try the wall? We had these in PE class, and I always had fun on them."

I pictured Vale racing to the top while the others in class stared in awe at his abilities.

"Rock wall it is then, Little Monkey. Let's get you fitted in a harness." It took a few minutes for the attendant to get him situated. In his excitement, Vale had a bit of trouble standing still, but finally managed to long enough to get him clipped in. I stood back and assessed everything and double-checked the carabiners. Granted, he wouldn't fall to the ground the way this was set up. I'd have hold of the other end of the rope, and I'd see to it that didn't happen. But still, safety first.

"All right, Little Monkey, climb until your limbs are weary." Excitedly, Vale hopped up and down and tried his luck at making monkey sounds. I. wasn't quite sure it was a success, but either way, he was happy and that's what mattered. Plus, he made me smile. Every move he made I had an eye on. Whether it be placing his hand or foot to a rock or glancing up to pick his next move, I tracked them all. I appreciated how he calculated each move and didn't just wildly jump around without considering where he'd land. When Vale reached the top he proudly rang the bell, his eyes danced as he mentally clapped for himself. Thank the rock wall gods he didn't physically do it.

Vale rappelled down and once both feet touched the ground he jumped just as excitedly as he had before he went up.

"Good job, Little Monkey. Where to next?" He was in character, so he didn't use his words, though I wasn't sure he'd completely immersed into subspace. But at least he'd tried and let go enough to feel a touch of the freedom associated with it. It'd likely take a few play sessions before he'd achieve it, considering how new this was to him.

He wandered toward the obstacle course and stood back and watched the pups and ferret run through it. I did appreciate the fact that the costume he made wasn't too revealing and he could easily move around in it. As much as I would have loved a sexier outfit in another setting, it probably wouldn't have gone over well here. Thankfully the shorts he made fell below his hips in lieu of the booty shorts most pet play outfits came with and he dressed it up with a cute furry vest. The monkey face was a basic mask with the eyes and mouth cut out, but the ears brought it together, and the tail was attached to his shorts. I appreciated that rather than having him wear an internal one. I was in no way against those and looked forward to being the lucky man who got to insert Vale's some hopeful day.

He made it through the maze and only fell once. Then he was up and over to the cat towers, nimbly maneuvering them. All the pets watched him, oohing and aahing. I thought for sure they'd clap at the end but they'd already re-emersed themselves in their pursuits. This little monkey was agile for sure and put on quite the show, and through it all his smile never faltered. He was so free and uninhibited having found his niche. I was correct in thinking pet play would be a welcome outlet for him. He hit the rock wall one more time before he planted himself on my lap in a bold, new move.

"Are you worn out, Little Monkey?" He nodded. "Would you like a bottle of water or a juice box?" My question was answered with another nod. I slid him onto the empty chair beside me and retrieved a juice box and a bottle of water from the nearby fridge. Figured whichever one he didn't drink I would.

"Which one, juice or water?" His eyes bobbed between the two before he finally pointed at the juice box. I popped a straw in and handed it over, seconds later he'd sucked it dry. "Would you like the water now?" Still in character, he shook his head no. "Let's sit for a few more minutes so you can unwind and relax." I slid my arm around the back of his chair, and he laid his head on my shoulder. I enjoyed this new layer of Vale. He hadn't been this open around me yet and I loved the personal touches, from sitting on my lap to laying his head against me.

I'd have offered to walk him back to his room but if I went anywhere near the staff quarters the cameras would likely catch me and then he'd be in trouble. Not worth the risk. Our time would come once we were both in Seattle.

When the seventh yawn rolled from him, it was time to bring our night to an end. "Sleepy Little Monkey, it's bedtime."

"But I'm comfy." He snuggled in deeper, nearly on my lap again.

"Me, too, and as much as I'd like to tuck you in, we both know that's not possible." How I wished he wasn't an employee of the cruise line right now. We'd return to my room and cuddle as we stared out at the moonlit night. Maybe we'd make love, maybe we wouldn't, but either way we'd be curled up together. This was harder than I thought it would be, and feelings were getting involved. I had it in my mind that casual dates while I was a passenger would be just fine and now here I was bidding him a reluctant goodnight.

"Sweet dreams, my cheeky little monkey." He'd taken my suggestion and created this adorable creature, and I was ever so proud of him. And happy to report the yawns meant good things, restful things. Likely a combination of all the hours he'd worked in conjunction with playtime. But I'd like to think that the playtime was most of it and would assist in his having a decent night's sleep.

We held hands as we strolled through the various rooms on our way to the main hallway.

"I'm this way," Vale hooked a thumb in the opposite direction from where my room was.

"Then this is where we say goodnight, my sweet boy." I gave him a brief kiss, not wanting to draw any unwanted attention. "I look forward to tomorrow's lunch date."

"Me, too. Goodnight, Jack."

"Goodnight, Monkey."

On the way back to my room, I wandered through the promenade deck window shopping. As I came upon a toy shop, an adorable monkey stuffie caught my eye and I knew it was meant for my boy. My boy worked hard, and he deserved a special treat. I envisioned him curled up with the little fluff ball in bed at night. But of course, being the nurturing Daddy I was, that wasn't all I walked out of the store with.

It was ridiculous how excited I was to share these gifts with Vale. I'd set one out each day at lunch for him to take back to his room. I made sure nothing was too big and unable to be hidden on his cleaning cart. I just wanted him to have some things to remind him of me once the cruise was over.

When I was back in my cabin I showered, ordered room service and settled in for a night of binge television. Being a workaholic definitely had its pros, but it came with a list of cons, too. Like the huge reality check I got when it hit me that I'd never given my past boys the attention that I was giving Vale and even in times like now when I sat down to start watching shows that I'd been meaning to watch for years. Now I actually had the time, though I'd still take on a new project here or there. Having a future with Vale slowly worked its way to the top of my list of importance.

As had catching up with my parents, too.

I was lucky in so many aspects. The fact that I was still able to do this at such a young age—semi-retire or vacation when I wanted. Things most people worked their entire lives, literally, for until the day they died while others dreamed of doing so when they reached retirement age. Then how many years did you have left after you retired? While I wasn't technically retired, being in my thirties with the ability to start living life the way it was meant to be was indeed a blessing.

One more day at sea then we would dock at our first stop on the island of Oahu. A day on the beach should help me relax. Maybe do some light shopping. Speaking of which, I logged onto the familiar pet site I'd purchased items from before and searched their gear. While the show I thought I wanted to watch played in the background, I laughed at the realization I wasn't one to sit still either. I shopped for a proper monkey suit for Vale. A boy with a vast amount of energy seemed to be just what I needed to pull me out of my slump.

Somewhere along the line, I lost myself while riding wave after wave of wrong boys. Something deep down inside me had awoken and I had Vale to thank for that. Though none of my relationships had ended in heartbreak, at least not by me, and I didn't remember any real tears from the boys that I'd spent any time with, they'd still ended. Granted, they weren't always meant to be relationships, just more playmates with benefits. I couldn't help but wonder if I had been selfish just by living my life my way I had.

It's funny how I came on board with the thought I'd work the entire time but since the moment Vale stormed into my room, he'd been my every waking thought. The list of places to take him and things to do had grown exponentially. It's crazy, these sudden changes in me and for all I knew Vale didn't even like any of the items I'd mentally listed for us to do. Or maybe he wouldn't want to spend that much time with me once he was home. But it was like my brain just couldn't stop.

On a bright note, I found the perfect outfit for him and had it shipped to my place. It would be waiting for him when he finally got back.

What if he signed another four-month contract? Would I be able to continually be apart from him for months on end?

My father always told me for him it was love at first sight the day he spotted my mother across the crowded room that fateful night. They both attended their senior prom but with other dates. They'd never really talked outside of class but knew who the other was. Their dates had wandered off and they took a chance and danced. From that moment forward they were inseparable.

While Dad attended college at UDub, Mom worked by choice. Mom wasn't inspired in a professional capacity. From a young age she'd dreamed of a family of her own and a house filled with children's laughter. So as soon as Dad graduated, they were married and moved into their first place together. Sadly, Mom suffered four miscarriages before finally carrying me, her fifth pregnancy, to term. She wanted more but her doctor warned her against it and even recommended a full hysterectomy before she left the hospital due to the damages caused from carrying me and during childbirth.

It broke her heart to know that she couldn't have any more, but she said the first time she held me and gazed into my eyes, all the pain was forgotten. At least in those moments. She called me her light, the one that brought her back from the dark and filled her days with joy. The one who made her whole again. I really had the best childhood. Yes, my father worked a lot, but again, I went with him once I was old enough to. What little bit of time he may have spent at home, he did everything in his power to ensure Mother and I always knew we were loved. We had everything we needed and honestly, I didn't remember my parents ever having had a single argument.

To this day, they still looked at each other like they hung the moon. Being married for more than forty years was amazing. I used to tease them when I was younger about being mushy and kissing and how gross it was but then as an adult, I grew to envy it. I never met two people more in love than my parents. Someday,

I hoped to have a love that strong. One that stood the test of time through the good and the bad. Knowing that the one person who held your heart was always there for you, and you for them.

I placed an order with catering for tomorrow's lunch to arrive promptly at noon, shut the computer down and ended up falling asleep with the TV on. Hadn't done that in forever, at home I barely turned the thing on.

Rejuvenated and ready for another day was how I woke up the next morning. Giddy to the point of having butterflies over seeing Vale again. Even though it had been less than twelve hours since we parted, it was far too long for me.

Meeting up twice a day, at least on the days that we weren't docked made the trip all that much better. I probably wouldn't get off at each island outside of Oahu because I'd previously been to them. But I knew Vale hadn't. During one of our conversations, he had mentioned he'd never been out of Washington, and I hoped to whisk him away on an island vacation someday.

So many plans, so little time.

Wasn't that the way it always went?

Chapter Seven
Vale

Was it odd that as soon as Jack opened the door I wanted to scream "Daddy" and run into his arms? Though I did still run into his open arms, I managed to keep the use of *Daddy* in check.

Daddy, handler, tomato, tohmato.

None of that was relevant.

"Little Monkey, it's far too long between our visits. Though I must admit I had a ton of fun last night."

"Me. too. But are you sure I didn't look ridiculous? I mean, the suit was super patchy, but I did my best with what I had. At least it didn't fall off." Thankfully I wore underwear underneath it, or it would have itched like hell. It needed to be washed, but I was afraid as soon as water touched it, it would either shrink or disintegrate.

"No, sweet boy, you did not look ridiculous. In case you didn't notice, all eyes were on you. Even the pets stopped playing to watch you. The crowd was enthralled with the silly monkey and on edge to see what he'd do next."

"I hadn't really picked a spirit animal but when I saw that costume, it all clicked into place. With the amount of energy coursing through me, a monkey swinging around, jumping from branch to branch seemed fitting. It was like a furry version of me."

Jack laughed. "Yes, I must say that choice was spot on, and I may have bought a thing or twelve for you for once you get back home. That is if you still want to see me when you get back."

Was it Jack's turn to exert uncertainty? "I do, I do, I do. I'm having so much fun, and you've opened a whole new world to me. Did you say you belong to a club where they have pet play?"

"Yes, the one in Seattle that's overseeing the dungeon, pet playroom, and littles' room on this very cruise as a matter of fact. It's called Blush."

"Do you think we could go there together sometime?"

"I would love nothing more. Now, have a seat and let's eat."

"Okay, Da-err." I nearly freaking said it. Never once had I called a single, solitary man Daddy. Hell, not even my own whom I'd never even met.

"Well, I think that near faux pas brought about our next topic of conversation. I would like to date you, exclusively, and in doing so I would be your handler, though I prefer to be called Daddy. But it's up to you how you wish to introduce or think of me. Whether that be your boyfriend, Daddy, partner, or your handler. Whatever makes you most comfortable. Point being, I have zero problems with you calling me Daddy. I know it's new to you, but please do whatever you're comfortable with. If you want the same thing as me, that is." A rambling Jack was too cute.

"I do. I'm still afraid of screwing it up. I'm not interested in dating anybody else. I absolutely love what we have, and I know it's my fault that we only get a little bit of time together, but I look forward to every second of it. Can we play again tonight?"

"I'd love nothing more, sweet boy. How did you sleep last night?"

"It was wonderful. As soon as I showered and lay down, I fell right to sleep. Which was a nice change, although usually I cat nap right when I lay down for an hour or two. But then I wake back up until around three or four, and then I'm down for round two." There goes my mouth again, running a million miles a minute and sharing stupid shit no one cares about. "Sorry," I sighed, frustrated. "Lost the brain-mouth filter." Jack smiled, completely unbothered by this. "I would have slept longer, I think, had our alarm clock not gone off. But in saying that, it was a solid five hours of sleep.

I didn't even get up to use the bathroom before the alarm clock blared."

"That's fantastic news I. knew pet play would be the right fit for you." Jack genuinely cared. It showed in every question. He truly wanted to know how I was. Not once had anyone asked that of me outside of Mom and Darcy. "Plus, I know you're working a lot of long, hard hours. Once we're both back on dry land, well, as dry as Seattle can get, it'll be a true test to see how pet play works for you. Do you plan to sign another contract with the cruise line when this is over?"

"Honestly, no. I'm aware Darcy pulled a lot of strings to get me this job. And while it is keeping me busy and out of trouble, which is a miracle, it's not the job for me. I'm starting to believe there will never be a right one." I'd gone through them like toilet paper. No matter how hard I tried I never fit anywhere.

No truer words had come from my mouth. Did that make me a loser? The fact that I didn't know what I wanted to do for the rest of my life? I had no interest in numbers. I was good with people except I usually pissed them off when I talked too much.

"Care to explain where that handsome head of your just ventured off to?"

"I don't want you to think I'm lazy because I'm really not and I know you're young and you've got your whole life planned and you know what you're gonna do and you've been doing it. But I've never had any plans. I've just kind of lived every day as best I could. I mean, my mom always worked, but she's a school-teacher. At times she had to work more than one job just to make ends meet and I hated that. I would love more than anything to some-day make enough money to pay all our bills, so she'd never have to work again. Although knowing her, she'd probably go crazy if she wasn't doing something at least part-time. For me I guess I haven't found where I fit. Noth-ing has stuck with me for more than a few months. I'm so scatterbrained that anything that takes a lot of concentration, like being a nurse or taking care of other people, wouldn't go over well."

"Don't sell yourself short, Little Monkey. You'll find your niche and it'll come to you when you least expect it. Or maybe not at all. But don't think less of yourself for that. It is my opinion that there's too much pressure put on youth these days to go to college, make money, buy a house, get married, have kids. I mean, those days are kind of behind us. While I get the point of making money to survive, it doesn't necessarily mean that there's one job for you for the rest of your life. Take me for example. Yes, I'm doing well, but I also have my hands in many pots. My money is invested in multiple avenues and businesses. Not one of them produces the same thing. They're all different startup companies. My interests lie all over the place."

"That's actually kinda cool, because you get to learn new stuff all the time by doing that. I mean, I suppose you research each one before you give them your money. At least I hope you do." Wasn't that how it worked, or did he have a separate wad of cash he just threw at a board to see where it landed? Disposable income or something like that.

Jack smiled again. "Sweet boy, I do. But I'm interested in what they do, just not in doing it myself. Does that make sense to you? I'd rather give them my money for them to keep doing it and then I'd move on to the next venture that caught my eye."

"Given the way my brain works, that's easier for me to absorb than just about anything else we've talked about. I don't know, I guess someday it'll come to me what I want to do. At least I hope it does or I'm gonna be living in my car when I get back home. That's a joke, by the way. My mom would never allow that to happen, but I refuse to mooch off of her for the rest of my life."

"From what you've told me about your mom, I can't see her thinking that poorly of you. Nor do I. Let's not spend what small amount of time we have together pondering things that can't be fixed now. Why don't we table that discussion for when you return then we can sit down and weigh your options. Does that sound fair?"

Jack was right, and clearly a list man, but it was engrained in me to always put my best foot forward. "It had been a dream of mine that there would come a time in life where I could afford to take Mom on vacation or a fun shopping trip. Just do something nice for her for a change." She'd more than earned it taking care of me.

Jack got a twinkle in his eye. "I understand that and I love the fact that you and your mom are as close as you are, as I am with my parents. I can't wait for you to meet them."

He had an uncanny knack for triggering choking fits in me. "You want me to meet your parents? Are you sure about that? Isn't that moving a bit too fast? You don't even know if you like me. You haven't had the pleasure of dealing with my highs and lows. I may drive you crazy." My heart raced and my palms sweated. The familiar panic increased. Could it be possible that someone actually liked me for more than my ass? Sixteen days. That's all Jack had with me. Was that enough time? Was it hot in here or was it just me?

"Deep breaths, sweet boy. And yes, I have thought that far ahead, and I've thought many other things. Based upon the fact that I just sent you into a deep, panic-filled spiral, I'm going to keep those thoughts to myself for now. But trust me, they're all good and I like you, Vale. A lot."

My face heated and I squirmed uncomfortably. "I um, I like you a lot, too. I'm just afraid of being me and driving you away."

"Sweetheart, it will take a lot more than endless energy to push me away. I have it, too, just my outlets differ from yours. You'll get there. We'll figure it out together."

"Promise?"

"I promise. Now, finish your lunch before the Daddy in me starts feeding you. Oh wait, I have something for you." Jack pulled a bag out from under the table and handed it to me. "Here."

"What is it?"

"Silly Monkey, open it up and see."

"Oh my God. Oh my God. Oh my God. It's a stuffie! He looks like my costume." I hugged him tightly. "The only other stuffies I had my mom got me when I was younger, and they'd seen better days. I'd been sleeping with them all my life, and even Mr. Bear lost his nose and one eye. It wasn't pretty, but I still loved him.

Thank you so much." Mom packed them away years ago with my baby stuff for safe keeping.

"You are very welcome. Now, what are you going to name him?"

I thought about it, then thought about it some more, then thought about it again. "Diego. Diego the Daredevil."

Jack laughed so hard I thought he might fall out of his chair. "Diego the Daredevil it is. All right, it's nice to meet you, Diego."

Diego sat perfectly on my lap, and I tucked a napkin into his tiny shirt in case I spilled anything. I didn't want him to get dirty. "He looks so cute with in his tiny rainbow t-shirt." None of the guys I dated ever gave me a gift. Not that I expected any, nor had I asked for one. This was super sweet of Jack. I'd sleep with him every night, even after Jack was gone.

"Why so sad, Little Monkey?"

"Nothing. Just bad thoughts that need to go away."

"Well, if they're bad thoughts about me, you must share them so I can make them go away. I just want you to be happy, Vale."

"I'm happy when I'm with you. I'm just afraid that once you step off the ship, that'll be the end of it." And away would walk my one chance at happiness. I guess having it briefly was better than not having it at all.

"Little Monkey, I promise you that will not happen. You'll see. I'm probably gonna send you so many emails that you block me.."

"Nope, not a chance. I'll be so excited that I'll be rushing through getting all my rooms done. Which probably won't go over well just so I can run to the computer and check for emails from my Da—"

"Little Monkey, what did I tell you?"

"Sorry. It's just gonna take a while for me to remember and to figure out why I want to call you Daddy when I've never had a boyfriend nor a Daddy before. For some reason, it just feels natural, and it keeps wanting to slip out."

"I'm a firm believer in there's a reason for everything. Don't question it, if it feels right go with it. If it doesn't, then don't. Either way, I'm still your boyfriend." Daddy got a smug look on his face.

Shit. Now I just thought out the whole word. Did that mean I had to say it? What's wrong with me?

"You've got that whole *lightbulb* look on your face. Did you have an epiphany of some sort?"

"You could say that." Jesus, what the fuck was wrong with me?

Lunch went by way too fast, and I'd returned to running my ass off, getting people towels, cleaning up spills, vacuuming carpets, all the fun stuff. *Not!* Through it all, my mind lingered on the parting kiss Jack and I shared.

Desperately, my heart strived to believe he was as into me as he said. Jack hadn't given me any reason to question that. In fact, he'd given me every reason to believe him. Unfortunately, my past dictated otherwise. Out of sight, out of mind and all that. Moving forward and leaving the past behind was the correct thing to do, but that was easier said than done. I was a work in progress, doing my best to push the demons aside and believe there was a chance for Jack and me.

How fast was too fast to fall for someone?

"Hey, lover boy." Darcy walked by and smacked the back of the head.

"Ouch! What did you do that for?"

"You were too busy daydreaming. Now, come on, let's go fold towels."

I'd taken Diego to our room and tucked him in before I met up with Darcy for the rest of our shift. Diego's adorable face poked out above the cover, waiting for me. It was nice that I'd have something from Jack while I finished my contractual obligation.

"You're not gonna sign on again, are you?" she asked when we got back to our room.

"No. I'm sorry. I appreciate all you did but honestly, I feel trapped. We can't talk to the passengers, there are days we don't even see the sun. It's just...a lot. But at least I gave it a try."

"You did and I get it. You're a hard worker and I'll give you an excellent recommendation to any future employer. *If* you don't screw up during the rest of your contract."

"I'll be good. Pinky swear." I held the finger up and she wrapped hers around mine. "Best friend promise."

With several weeks to go, I had plenty of time to piss her off, though I'd do my best not to. If anyone could handle me it was Darcy. The job wasn't hard, just time consuming and quite honestly, lonely and boring at times, but at least I'd have a bit of money in the bank while I looked for another job later.

Jack and I had made a date to meet in the playroom at the same time as last night, and he said he'd wait if I ran late. He did understand that my job came first, and I was at the mercy of it. How anyone did this for years on end 'd never understand.

I clock watched all night and drove myself mad. When it was finally time to clock out, Darcy and I returned to our room, and she helped me get changed into my monkey suit.

Ha–ha, a monkey suit that didn't have a tie. I cracked myself up.

"I envy you, Vale," Darcy said as she helped me with my mask. "I'm not brave enough to go down to the littles' room, and even if I did I couldn't do anything more than watch. There's no way to cover my face like you can."

"I hate that for you, Darcy, I just want you to be happy." My heart ached for her.

She shrugged. "It sounds like Jack is really into you. Just make sure and tell him if he does anything wrong or if he hurts you that he'll have to deal with me."

"LOL, my big, bad, protector Darcy, but I'll tell him. Thanks for helping me get ready."

I kissed her cheek and off I went, speed walking down to the room. Right as I entered there stood Jack, talking to the same attendant from last night.

"Hello, Monkey, do you need help getting strapped in tonight?" the attendant asked and I glanced at Jack to see what he wanted me to do.

"Maybe just show me one more time how to do it so I can make sure I don't miss anything. Then, after tonight, we should be able to handle it," Jack winked at me as he replied.

I was ready to run and jump and swing and wondered if Blush had something specifically for monkeys. Jack would know, or maybe we could find a place with a playground. I used to love to swing from those bars overhead. I missed those days and thought they were long gone. How silly it was of me to believe I was too old to have that kind of fun again.

Focused on future events, I hadn't realized they'd suited me up and I was ready to go until Jack touched my shoulder.

"Are you with me? Monkey?" My nod soothed his concern. Was I supposed to talk when in costume? I guess I did when I was done last night but I'd ask Jack later. I was inn and out of a weird, floaty dream state when I played the first time. Like slipping in and out of a headspace that was me yet not me. If that made any sense? Like warm and fuzzy and content, kinda hard to explain. Maybe that is the subspace I read about online.

Off I went into the awaiting maze before me. It was fun to be this free, no worries and Jack below prepared to catch me if I fell. This was all for me. I'm sure some people at the end of a shift only wanted to relax, but I had all this energy pent-up inside me that needed released. This was perfect, a way to be me without being the me who annoyed everyone. I was one with the monkey, moving gracefully like the wind from object to object. The monkey didn't have to think about clocking in or if the bed sheets were perfect and the towels were folded. Monkey served monkey only and I loved it.

There was a certain freedom that came along with adopting such a free persona. And to have the right person to share that with? Nothing compared and that alone had its own freedom to let go and be me while someone else worried about what came next.

I wondered if there was a job for professional obstacle course or playground testers 'cause I was pretty damn good at this. Swinging on newly erected sets to see how they held up, if they had a net below to catch me, I'd be down for that. Ooh, I wonder if Jack would take me bungee jumping? He'd probably freak out and worry I'd get hurt. It was nice to have somebody else to worry about me besides Mom. She needed a Vale brain break. There came a point in your life where you needed to find the one that loved you enough to worry.

Had I found that in Jack?

Whoa, Vale, don't get ahead of yourself.

One could always wish...

Chapter Eight
Jack

Going ashore without Vale was harder than I'd anticipated. Sunning on the beach alone wasn't for me. How was I going to handle the long months apart that lay ahead for us? I brushed off the sand and strolled down the row of shops, hoping a trinket or two to treat my boy with would catch my eye. In the end, I snagged a couple of goodies but midway through the day I'd had enough and returned to the ship. I took a chance and shot off a text to Vale, not positive when or if it would go through.

Me: Called it a day, back in my room. Pop in if you're nearby.

After I stored his gifts in an empty suitcase with the others, it was time to shower the salt and sand away. What I didn't expect to find when I stepped out wearing only a towel around my waist was my sweet monkey jumping on the bed.

"Daddy!" He squealed and ran across the room to me. "I missed our lunch date."

"Me, too, but having you call me Daddy more than made up for it."

"Sorry, it just came out." He snuggled into my arms. This was what I needed. Instantly, my soul settled once I held him.

"Don't apologize, I loved it." Shit, my towel slid off. "My turn to say sorry."

Vale giggled and slid his hands down and grabbed my ass. "Don't apologize," he used my words on me. "I'm enjoying this."

"Cheeky boy."

Vale stood back and let his hungry gaze roam over every inch of me. I felt exposed and adored at the same time, cherished even. This was the most attention he'd paid to my body. Perfectly fit, I was not. A six-pack and all the goodies guys ogled wasn't a part of my physique and based upon Vale's reaction he was pleased with me as I was. Every interaction with this sweet boy turned the lock on my heart tighter, in his favor. He'd soon own it and the key.

"My Daddy is yummy."

"Yummy? Not sure that's ever been used to describe me. But yes, I am *your* Daddy and yours alone, and as long as you're pleased that's all that matters to me." I drew my sassy boy in for a heated kiss. "Be careful, you don't want to start things you don't have time to finish."

"Grr," he growled. "This is becoming increasingly difficult, isn't it?"

"It is, dear boy. What is it you desire right now? For Daddy to take care of you and make you come?" I rubbed against him, and he was just as hard as I was. This may be pushing the envelope given we'd not discussed copulating, but we both had those pesky erections to take into consideration.

"That's not fair, Daddy." It appeared the nick-name that he'd lovingly adopted was best suit-ed for manipulation. Not sure how I felt about that, but he was cute as hell, and I'd table that discussion for another day.

"Then what are you suggesting, sir?" My wicked, flirtatious side emerged in preparation of the salacious devouring of my dear Vale.

"Well, it's not much later than our usual lunchtime dates. And I'm guessing we both al-ready ate. And even if we hadn't, food wouldn't get here in time. So maybe we just do a quick dine and dash of each other?"

"I like your way of thinking, but only if you're completely comfortable with that, Vale. Noth-ing ever has to happen that you don't want to, and nothing will ever be expected of you."

"I know, and I appreciate that and it's part of why I want this to happen. I believe this, what-ever is happening between us, means more to us both. It's not just a fleeting moment on a cruise ship."

"Vale, you are correct. But remind me when we're done, I have another gift for my sweet boy."

"You don't have to buy me things to be with you, Jack."

Back to Jack are we? Time to flip that shit back around.

"Let me see, what did someone else in this cabin just say? Oh yeah, I know, and I appreciate that and it's part of why I want this to happen. Two can play the honesty game and the only way a long-distance relationship will work for us is to keep that in mind." There was so much more to say but the way he touched me clouded my mind.

Vale ran his fingers through the hair on my chest. "I do, but whatever will we do with my clothes?" Vale batted his lashes then turned serious. "I can't get them wrinkled because I still have to work after this."

"Let me do the honors." Piece by piece, I disrobed my adorable boy and carefully draped each item over a nearby chair. If anything wrinkled, I'd run a quick iron over it for him.

"Look at you, such a beautiful boy. I always enjoy unwrapping a gift." The gift of a beautiful boy, that was. "Now, whatever shall I do with him?" Vale had been so good, not fiddling as he stood there—until I asked that. His beautiful cock bobbed as he hopped up and down.

"Make me come, Daddy. Please?"

Dear God, this boy would be my undoing. He would break me and put me back together in a mold that suited him, and I couldn't wait to enjoy every sexy moment of that. Was it possible to have a teenager's libido again? I laid him back on the bed and gazed down at his beautiful body lying amongst the starched linens. How perfectly he belonged there. I firmly gripped the base of my shaft to stave the pending release. I hadn't been this, for lack of a better term, prematurely active since my early teen years. Everything about Vale was beautiful inside as well as out and that combination was lethal.

Unfortunately, time wasn't on our side today, and I couldn't spend the limited amount worshiping his body the way he deserved. This was gonna be quick and normally quick meant dirty, but I wasn't about to diminish how important this was to us both. My lips trailed kisses down his torso as I gently spread his legs and knelt between them. I wanted Vale to feel, not think, and enjoy the moment while it lasted. My shaft eagerly bobbed, awaiting its turn, but it could wait. It was important that Vale saw that he was first with me.

When I took his cock head into my mouth, he moaned and arched up. Drawing more of those illicit sounds from him was my new goal, along with making him scream my name as he came. Up and down his shaft my lips slid, and my tongue swirled around every inch of it. Over the vein and under the crown, down along the underside.

"Daddy," he panted. I held his hips firmly in place as they tried to thrust up again. It didn't take long before my eager boy's cock throbbed in my mouth, and with a guttural moan he came. I devoured every drop then hovered above him and pressed my lips to his. Vale wrapped his hand around my cock and stroked. My plan was to just let him have it all and take care of myself later. But who was I to deny my boy this? He wished to touch me, to take care of me and I'd longed for it to be his hand and not mine, so I'd let him have his way.

"Baby." I gazed into his beautiful eyes. He stroked harder, faster. Given my current mind-set and the pent-up way I was before we even began, I'd be no better than him at holding out. I'd make it up to him another time when we could enjoy making love all night long. As my release barreled forth, I pressed my lips to his and thrust my tongue inside his mouth and came harder than I had in a long time. Then again, I'd been the only one to touch me for, Jesus, who knew how long? But it wasn't all about the act so much as it was who you performed it with and in this case, being with Vale only served to intensify and elevate it to a level I hadn't reached before. I knew the reason behind it, but I wasn't ready to admit it to myself, nor say it aloud and risk scaring Vale away. He was already unsure and far too important to me to fuck this up.

"Let me grab a towel and I'll get us cleaned up." I was only gone a second and in that time, Vale was already mid-dressing. I wiped the come from his chest as well as the bit that got on me and tossed the towel across the room toward the bathroom. An uneasy feeling shot through me at how quiet Vale had become. Had this been wrong?

"Is everything okay, Little Monkey?"

Downward his gaze remained as he briefly nodded. Not. Good.

"Wait, I have something for you." I ran over to the closet and pulled out the item I wanted to give him today and handed him the bag.

"Really? For me?" He shook his head as if in disbelief. "This is usually the point where I get ghosted, just it's the first time I'm walking away with a parting gift."

"Sweetheart, I'm not dumping you and we need to shift your mindset on that. I understand this," I gestured between us, "hasn't been long. But I'm doing my best to prove to you that I've meant what I've said. What more do you need to understand I'm all in?"

He reached into the bag and pulled the gift out and tears welled in his eyes. "You got me a monkey backpack. He matches the stuffy you gave me."

"Yes, he does." I wiped the tears away. "Please don't cry, Little Monkey. What we just did was beautiful and only the beginning. We will have the rest of our lives to do that and more." I feared he still didn't believe me. "Vale." I lifted his chin for him to see the sincerity in mine at my next words. "I'm falling for you. Hard and fast. I'm trying not to scare you away with this revelation, but I can't help how I feel." Before he could say a word, I drew him to me and pressed my lips to his, conveying all I could through our kiss.

"You–you mean it?" he stuttered, clutching the backpack to his chest. "I mean, you get me, and that's what scares me even more, because nobody ever has. And then you buy me stuff, which isn't necessary, but nobody's ever done that either. It just makes my head spin. And then I worry. And then my heart hurts and I don't want my heart to hurt. It's hurt too much already." He rambled on in that adorable way of his, though I knew the words hurt for him to say.

"My Sweet Monkey, I would soon cut my own heart from my chest before I hurt yours."

"Oh, Daddy." He whimpered and pressed tighter against me. "I hate that I have to return to work after this. I just want to be with you all the time. It's gonna be so hard when you leave."

"I know, but we'll talk as often as we can, I promise." Speaking with a conviction I barely held took all I had. But I was the Daddy here and it was my job to calm and reassure my boy. "I'll probably drive you insane with the number of messages and emails I'll send you. Waiting to hear from you will make me crazy."

Finally, a cute giggle escaped. "Okay. Thank you for my backpack. It's perfect but unfortunately, I have to get back to work."

"No pouting," I tugged his bottom lip free. "I love these lips so no abusing them. Tonight, I'll wait in the usual spot for my silly monkey." Vale pressed his lips to mine once more and then he was out the door and took a piece of my heart with him. While I was a bit sad, I was elated that I'd brought a parting smile to my boy's face. Hopefully, it brightened his day and would help get him through his long work shift.

The remainder of the afternoon was spent lounging around my room, rotating between work related things and internet scrolling. My thoughts were filled with all things Vale. I received an email notification that his new costume shipped but alas, it would wait for weeks before his contract ended, and I could see the little cutie in it. Was it wrong of me to hope that he left when I did? But I couldn't do that to him. This was his employment and his friend got him the job. Being selfish wasn't who I was, nor was that fair to Vale.

For dinner, I dined on the balcony in my room as opposed to going to the restaurant. And instead of binge-watching mindless television, though I'd never gotten anywhere with that series, I instead picked up a book. With a breeze in my hair and the warmth of the sun, I got lost in the worlds of mythical beasts.

This page-turning novel with dragons who hid amongst the humans in secondary personas but could shift into their true forms in the blink of an eye captivated me. Sent to Earth to guard the lost treasures that had been hidden here from their realm thousands of centuries before. The author was truly gifted and had a way with words to where you felt you stood beside these magical beasts while they battled evil. Though I enjoyed the tale, I was all too happy to set the book down when my alarm went off to go meet my sweet Vale.

"Daddy," he whispered as we embraced.

"Yes, Sweet Monkey, I'm here. Ready to play?" He wiggled out of my arms and hopped over to the harness area. "I'll take that as a yes. Let's get you suited up." I enjoyed learning how to do this myself. It would serve us well in the future. Not all our time would be spent indoors as I had a plethora of outings planned for Vale.

Off he went, scaling up the wall like the monkey he was. The boy was brilliant, the course engrained in memory as he glided over each hold with ease. Tonight, he was on a mission to climb to the top without the aid of the footholds. They were there if he needed them, but his iron will and determination had him relying on his upper body strength to reach the top and sure enough, when he rang the bell all eyes were on him.

"Way to go, Monkey!" the handlers shouted as the pets' padded claps rang out.

But monkey wasn't done. He rappelled down and yanked at his harness. "I get the hint, little imp." After he was free and clear of all restraints, he bounded over to the obstacle course and dove into the tunnels and raced the pups through. His energy drew the other pets to follow. Round and round they went until the pups tuckered out and monkey moved onto the cat scratcher.

Patiently I waited for my little monkey to tucker out. Hell, I'd only watched, and I was exhausted. Imagine having that much excess energy? I could've repainted my condo already.

"Ready for bed, monkey?" A big yawn rushed forth before he could reply. "I'll take that as a yes. Time to go."

The brief kiss we shared in the hall before parting wasn't enough.

How could I get more time with my boy before this trip was over?

Chapter Nine
Vale

"Stop fidgeting." Darcy was not at all happy with me. Lost in fuzzy daydreams of my Daddy, I wasn't paying attention and nicked my finger on the razor blade while we stocked the supply room. "You're lucky it didn't go any deeper and require stitches. Showing up in the infirmary would be bad for both of us."

True, plus the amount of paperwork Darcy would have to fill out was ridiculous.

"Sorry, Darcy." Ugh, generally mistakes were made when my body moved faster than my brain. This time I wasn't moving at all.

"Can't have you wrecking the towels and toilet paper with your blood, now can we?"

"Ha-ha. You're so funny." But she was right, one of the boxes was a bit...caked in it. Thought I'd nicked an artery there for a minute.

"I'll open the boxes and you stock the shelves. Deal?"

"Ugh, deal." Relegated to stock boy.

"Okay, brat. Spill it. You're never this quiet unless something's wrong. Do I need to kick your new Daddy's ass? Has he hurt you?"

"God no, he's...perfect. Like, literally." The end of the cruise was nearing. The passengers visited the last island today and then we'd embarked upon the journey home.

"Then what's the issue?"

"No man has ever been this nice, this caring and so wonderful to me. I'm just afraid once he steps ashore the dream ends."

"Let's recap, shall we?" When I didn't respond, she continued. "This is your longest relationship to date, is it not?"

"It is and thank you for pointing out what a loser I am."

"Not what I'm doing. Jack has showered you with gifts with no expectation for sex. Correct?"

"Well, there's been a little."

"Nothing more than what you do to yourself. In *our* shared shower, I might add."

Fucking thin walls.

"Yeah, I've heard you and no amount of bleach can cleanse that from my brain." She shuddered.

"Is this speech going somewhere or is your goal to embarrass me?" I mean, really. "Make your point and move on, woman."

"My point is that the man is on vacation, yet he spends every second he can with you. My god, he didn't get off the ship but one time and we stopped at four islands. He dines you, gives you gifts, plays Daddy to your monkey and yet he's asked for nothing in return. I think he's the real deal, Vale. You've got a chance at your forever while the rest of us are destined to spend our lives alone."

Maybe she had a point.

"Now buck up, little man, and pull your head out of your ass before you lose the best thing that's ever happened to you." Darcy tossed a roll of toilet paper at me, narrowly missing my head.

"Darcy, your Mommy is out there somewhere waiting for you. I know she is." How selfish had I been? Focused on me and my insecurities while forgetting my best friend was hurting. She'd tucked herself away on a cruise ship to avoid the pain. But what if her special someone waited to be found back in Seattle and Darcy hid too long and missed her?

When we got done with the room, I texted Daddy.

Me: *Daddy, I think I hurt Darcy's feelings.*

Daddy: *What did you do, Monkey?*

Me: *Typical pity party for one starring Vale…Ugh.*

Daddy: *Need more intel than that to figure this out.*

Me: *Sorry. Just whining and Darcy got really sad, and I know it's because she is lonely and wants a Mommy.*

Daddy: *Oh. Well, I can't help with that from here, but I might be able to once we're all back in Seattle.*

Me: *Really?*

Daddy: *No promises so don't tell her but I've got a few ideas. Maybe she can go to Blush with us some time.*

Me: *Thank you, Daddy. I'll see you tonight.*

Daddy: *I can't wait, Little Monkey.*

Each day, Daddy gave me a gift during our lunch date. I had so many new, wonderful things yet I'd never given him anything. Deciding to make him something special so every time he saw it he'd think of me had been a challenge, but when an idea finally presented itself I knew Daddy would love it.

"What are you doing with those scraps?" Darcy asked one night when I had them sprawled across our shared desk. I'd just returned from pet play with Daddy.

"Making a present for Jack. I want him to have something to remember me by. Can you take my picture, please?" I posed while Darcy snapped away then we went through them together to find the perfect one and I printed it out.

"This is really cute, Vale. I like crafts and glitter. Lots of glitter." Darcy's little side slipped out. "Can I help?"

"Sure." I pushed some scraps over to her and she got to work on her own project. Her tongue poked out as she concentrated hard. Adorable was the best way to describe it as she hummed along to the tune inside her head.

I hoped this gift would be as special to Daddy as it was to me. It was kinda wonky, I was no artist for sure, but it was the part of me he understood. Maybe he would use it, maybe not, but either way I tried my best and that's all I could do.

"Can you help me with the glitter? I'm not allowed to do it by myself." Darcy's big eyes peered up at me, pleading for a yes. I wasn't quite sure why she wasn't allowed to use glitter, but I hadn't done enough research on littles to fully understand or comprehend their mindset.

"Sure. Show me where you want it and I'll sprinkle it on there for you." With every dot of glue she placed we played a game of chase as I sprinkled the glitter on it for her. She clapped and sang her silly little tune as we hopped along her canvas. Finally, I got it. Having a little was like a babysitting job, though I wasn't getting paid for it. But it didn't matter—we had fun and that was the best part. It was nice for the two of us to spend this time together when we weren't working our day job. The only work we were doing was having fun.

"Here, Vale," she said when she was done, "I made this for you to put on your fridge at home and 'member me when I'm far away on the big boat."

"Darcy, you're my best friend and I'll never forget you. I love you."

"I love you, too, Vale. I seepy. I'm gonna put on my jammies." She hopped up, grabbed her PJs off the foot of her bed and skipped into the bathroom to change. I kind of looked forward to being around some littles when Daddy took us to the club. I hadn't shared that with Darcy yet, I'd probably wait till it was time to go, or at least until we got off the ship. She'd be excited. I wondered if a monkey was allowed in the littles' room.

The next day for lunch nerves hit as I headed to Daddy's cabin for the last time. Well, the last time he'd be in there. I still had to do a thorough clean once the passengers were gone. The gifts were wrapped in some paper I found and tucked away on my cart where nobody would see. I knocked and called out, "Cabin steward," like always and Daddy let me in. Once I pushed my cart to the side, I ran right into his open arms.

"There's my sweet boy. How's your day been?" Daddy cradled me and pressed his lips to the top of my head.

Safe.

That's how I always felt with him.

"Same as every day. Boring, but busy. Does that make any sense? Can you use those two words in the same sentence? Kinda like an oxymoron." My own brain confused me, so it likely had the same effect on him.

Daddy laughed. "It makes sense to me, Silly Monkey. Come and sit. Let's have lunch."

"Oh, wait. I have a present for you." I dug it out of the cart and took a deep breath to calm myself. The only people in my life I'd ever given gifts to were Mom and Darcy.

"Here, Daddy. Sorry. I'm not very good at wrapping."

"You didn't have to get me anything, Sweet Boy. But thank you." He unwrapped it and as soon as he saw what was inside, he smiled wide. "Oh, Little Monkey. This is perfect and such a cute picture of you. Did you get Darcy to take it?"

"Yes, she said it's cute, so I hope it's okay. I got to play with her little last night, it was fun."

"I bet it was. This picture frame, it's made from a piece of your costume, isn't it?"

"Yup. So is the notebook." I'd made Daddy a journal with paper inside and the outside was covered in the fur from my costume with two silly googly eyes glued on the front. A silly monkey from his silly monkey. The picture frame matched, and I'd put the picture Darcy took inside it. That way every time he looked at it he'd remember me.

"I washed those pieces of fur really good before I used them. I didn't want you to get sick from all the dust."

"So thoughtful is my Little Monkey. Thank you, Vale." Daddy tugged me onto his lap and kissed me, then nibbled my neck and tickled me until I giggled. "I think my Little Monkey needs to eat now."

"Yes, Daddy." I was comfy, and safe, and didn't want to get up. But I didn't want to upset Daddy.

"Tomorrow is our last day together, Little Monkey. I want to do something special."

"I'm honestly to the point where I don't care if I get in trouble. This is ridiculous having to steal time away like we're doing something illegal. Granted, where my job is concerned I kind of am. But it's not fair, Daddy." I sounded like a petulant child and had I been standing I likely would've stomped my foot in protest.

"I agree, Sweet Boy, but rules are rules and I suppose they have them in place for a reason. I wish you could sleep over, but I almost prefer the idea of us waiting to take that step until we're both on solid ground. It's kind of humorous, two grown out of the closet men hiding. Both of which have been out of for quite a long time. At least I have been."

"I knew at a young age I was gay, and my mom knew, too. I never had to say the words to her, it was just expected I'd bring home a boyfriend. You'll like her, my mom. She's a wonderful woman, so amazing and patient."

"She sounds like a dream, and I can't wait to meet her."

"Unfortunately, I have to get back to work. Tonight will be our last pet play scene. I guess they're not gonna have it tomorrow night since they need to tear everything down." What would I have as an outlet for the next fourteen weeks? I thought we were allowed to use the gym and that climbing wall would stay. I'd have to check with Darcy and see if that was open to crew members.

"I'm sorry, Little Monkey, but I promise to make all of that up to you once we can be together the right way. Then we can monkey around all the time."

"You're funny, Daddy, and I've come to accept that the monkey is my spirit animal."

"Glad to hear it." Daddy stood and held his hand out to me to help me up. "Until tonight, my sweet boy." He pressed his lips to mine. Every time was like the first and my Daddy really knew how to kiss.

"See you tonight, Daddy."

As soon as the door shut behind me it was like someone kicked me in the stomach. This really sucked, there was no other way to put it and no way I wouldn't slip into a deep depression for the next three and a half months.

With the cruise coming to an end, the cabin calls slowed down which allowed Darcy and I to break away earlier today than we had been. We decided to take dinner back to our cabin and watch a movie until I had to go meet Daddy.

"I'm really sorry you have to say goodbye to your Daddy tomorrow, Vale. I don't like it when you're sad."

"I don't like it either, but I don't want you to think I don't appreciate what you've done for me, because I do. How much longer do you think you're gonna be able to sell your life to the sea goddess for?"

She shrugged. "I don't know. I mean, it pays well. Beats the hell out of the job market in Seattle right now and going home to an empty house. I guess we'll see how it goes while we're on break. I'm not gonna say I'm not open to finding another local job, because I'm not. The issue is the fact I don't know what I really want to do."

That I understood more than she knew having just had the same conversation with Daddy.

Darcy and I snuggled underneath her favorite blanket, like we had so many times throughout our childhood and when my alarm clock went off, she helped me get ready to meet Daddy for our last pet play session.

What I didn't expect to find was Daddy standing there waiting for me with a big gift bag in hand.

"Hello, Little Monkey. Are you ready to play?" I bounced up and down, my head bobbing with me and pointed at the bag. "Oh, this? This is for my special monkey and his little friend, Darcy."

My Daddy was so sweet, he even thought of Darcy. That's what a true Daddy was, a man who not only cared about his boy, but his boy's friends and family. He wanted to meet my mom and have me meet his parents, too. That had to mean something, right? Not gonna lie, it was a lot and a bit scary, but it was also amazing to know that somebody liked me enough to show me off like that.

At the end of the night, all the pets gathered around. I wasn't sure what was going on until they started hugging each other. Next thing I knew, they hugged me, too, and told me how much fun they had watching me. That filled my heart beyond words. I had been afraid I looked like a fool while playing, though during which I hadn't cared. Flying, free floating as I hovered above my body, watching as I let go and had the time of my life. Knowing Daddy was there watching me was like wrapping the entire event in a pretty bow.

When I got back to the room, Darcy was still awake but hopped right up when she saw I had a gift bag. "What's in the bag? What did your Daddy get you?"

"Us."

"Huh?" She cocked her head to the side.

"Daddy said the stuff in the bag was for both of us." When I looked inside there were two bags, one marked for me and one for Darcy.

She dug into hers with all the vigor of a kid on Christmas Day. "Look, Vale, crayons and coloring books, and an axolotl squishmallow. I love her so much," she squeezed the rainbow and teal stuffie to her chest. "What did you get?"

"I got a new stuffy giraffe and a coloring book with animals and coloring pencils."

"Your Daddy is silly. He did all of this for us. Tell him I said, thank you, please." She began flipping through the pages of her new coloring book while I fired off a text to Daddy.

Me: *Thank you so much for all our goodies. Darcy is already coloring in her new book and is glued to her stuffie.*

I took a picture of her and sent it to him.

Daddy: *She's adorable. I'm glad you both like your gifts.*

Me: *We love them and thank you so much for including Darcy. She's been sad and you made her smile.*

Daddy: *Glad to help but did my boy smile too?*

Me: *I can't stop.*

I flipped the phone around and took a picture of my face and sent it to Daddy.

Me: *See*

Daddy: *Yes I do. There's my Sweet Monkey.*

Me: *Send me a picture of you please and make sure I take one of us together tomorrow for my screen saver.*

A couple seconds later a picture of Daddy in bed without a shirt on came through. I couldn't wait until I could fall asleep with my head on his fuzzy chest.

> Me: *My Daddy's so handsome.*

> Daddy: *And my boy is so beautiful but it's past his bedtime.*

> Me: *Night, Daddy.*

> Daddy: *Night, Sweet Boy.*

Chapter Ten
Jack

"Don't cry, Little Monkey. I promise when you get off the ship I'll be there waiting for you. Until then, we can email, text, and video chat as often as you can." Jesus, this was the hardest fucking thing I'd ever had to do, leaving my boy. Brought together by a random twist of fate and one I'd forever thank those very fates for.

"I'm going to miss you so much, Daddy." Vale sniffled. "This sucks."

"Yes, it does but, Vale," he glanced up at me. "I love you, and I promise you're the only one for me. My perfect boy."

He burst into tears, crying harder than he had been. "I. Love. You. Too," he got each word out between sobs.

This was killing me.

"I'll sneak out on deck and wave goodbye."

I had zero doubts he would do that, and I'd comb the crowd until I found him.

"Remember, my love, this isn't goodbye forever, it's merely a goodbye, I'll see you soon." But damned if it didn't feel otherwise. My boy washed his face and with a final kiss he was off, and I returned to packing. Far too soon it was done, and my thoughts were once again consumed with all things Vale. At least once I was gone, he wouldn't have to sneak around, breaking rules and he'd have more time to spend with Darcy.

Speaking of Darcy, a meeting with Ms. Vivienne, the owner of Blush and the very one who'd sponsored this event, was in order. Vivienne and I went way back, before club days. Two young college kids with big dreams and delusions of grandeur, though not as delusional as we'd once thought given our dreams had become a reality. Not many were as lucky as we were, but I was a silent partner, in finance only in Blush, and wishing my friend all the happiness I'd found in my boy, and the best way to do that was to find her a girl of her own.

I believed I'd just met her perfect little.

I woke in the middle of the night as soon as I heard the door open and close, and the sweet voice I longed to hear whispered, "It's me, Daddy. Don't be scared."

"Sweet boy, what are you doing here? It's three a.m."

"I know, but we're collecting all the luggage and of course I have my rooms to do, but I wanted to run in and give you a kiss and a big hug. I'm gonna miss you so much." Vale wrapped his arms around my neck.

"I'm gonna miss you, too, sweetheart, more than you know." I tugged him down onto the bed with me and started tickling him.

"Daddy! Daddy! I still have a bunch of luggage to pick up, but I just couldn't come by and grab yours and not say anything."

"Well, I'm glad you did. I don't want you to get into trouble, but one last stolen moment makes my heart happy."

"I love you so much, Daddy."

"I love you, Little Monkey." We kissed for a few minutes before our time ended abruptly. At this point it wasn't worth trying to sleep anymore, not that I had been. I got up and dressed and went to breakfast in my designated area, leaving a hearty tip for the staff before I disembarked. Two long hours it took to get off the ship given the amount of passengers doing the same thing. As soon as I was, I felt my boy's eyes on me and glanced up to scan the crowd out on the deck. I didn't dare yell his name because everyone around him was a crew member but as soon as I spotted him, I blew him a kiss and tapped my heart. My way of letting him know I loved him, and he did the same.

I made my way to the luggage carousel and once I'd collected mine, met the Uber driver at the pick-up stand. The drive home was somber. I'm sure most were happy to be on their way home, reflecting on the fantastic cruise they'd had, ready to share it with their friends and family. For me, the fact I'd left a piece of my heart on that ship and only one person could bring it back to me was a somber memory.

Through the heavy Seattle traffic, we finally got across the river and into Bellevue and pulled up in front of my building. The driver kindly helped me out with my luggage and as soon as I stepped inside the elevator, the loneliness hit me. Through all these months I'd spent alone, I never felt lonelier than I did then. Now that I had someone to share my life with, I wanted to. No longer content to be the bachelor I once was.

I unpacked, started a load of laundry and took inventory of what was in the cupboards and fridge, then placed a grocery delivery order. It was too early for a glass of wine, though I really wanted one. Instead, I dialed my mother.

"How's my world traveling son today?"

"Well, good morning to you, too, Mother Dearest. Didn't travel the world so much as down to the Hawaiian Islands and back up."

"Do you hit any storms? Have any fun? Meet a man?"

My mother the match maker, always hoping to pair me up.

"No storms, had fun, met the love of my life." And I left it at that, knowing full well that her wheels were spinning like a mother fucker right then.

"What? No? Don't tease your mother. You know I have a bad ticker."

"Woman, you are such a liar. You're in better health than I am."

"Tsk. That is not true. So, when do we get to meet this man that stole your heart?"

"Ugh, therein lies the problem. Vale is one of the crew and only sixteen days into a four-month contract. But Mom, you're gonna love him." Without out a doubt, she'd fall for him as quickly as I had but in a motherly way.

"Sounds like my son needs a mother's ear and maybe even a hug."

"Both, please. I was thinking about coming up this weekend."

"Repack your bags, grab the groceries I know you just ordered, and get your ass out here."

Hardy laughter burst from me. My mother was something special. Gods how I loved that woman. "All right, Mommy Dearest. I'm doing some laundry now. How about I head your way tomorrow?"

"Let me know when you get on the ferry, and I'll tell your father to fire up the grill and throw the meat on."

"I love you, Mom."

"I love you, too, baby boy. We'll see you tomorrow. Can't wait to hear all about your mister."

One more call to make.

"Well, well, well, if it isn't the elusive Mr. Jack Barrett. Back from your cruise already?" My assistant's chipper voice reminded me of one of the many reasons why I'd hired her over a decade ago.

"Hello, Diana. Did I miss anything? The building burn down?" Even though I checked in with her while I was on the cruise, and of course, she reminded me there was nothing to worry about, I still felt the urge to call.

"You know the answer to that, Jack. Will you be gracing us with your presence tomorrow?"

"Do you need me to?" She didn't, but part of being a good boss was asking.

"Hmm, if I didn't know any better, I would think you were trying to get out of work. Did the workaholic have some sort of epiphany while out to sea?" Ever the inquisitive friend she was.

"Something like that. I was thinking about heading out to Whidbey for a few days to spend some time with my parents."

"That sounds like a great idea. I've got a couple of contracts for you to review. I'll send them via email, and you can sign and send them back. Otherwise, everything's running smoothly. Sooo..." She drug the word out and I knew exactly what would come next. "Did you meet anyone special?"

Sometimes I swore Diana and my mother were of the same brain. "As a matter of fact, I did."

"Don't lie to me. Jack, I've worked for you long enough to know you better." That woman could sniff out bullshit a mile away.

"Now, would I lie to my favorite girl?"

"Cute, but seriously?"

"Yes, seriously, I met someone. His name is Vale. He's part of the crew and he's still under contract with the cruise line for a couple of months while I'm back here wallowing in loneliness." Oh no, my turn for a pity party.

"Okay, who is this and what have you done with Jack Barrett? Do I need to call the authorities?"

"Ha-ha-ha. There's a reason why I've kept you on the payroll, Diana, it's your witty charm and subservient demeanor." That latter of which she was not.

"Subservient my ass. No, it's my ability to put up with you, grouchy pants, and you know it."

"No denying that, although I've felt a change in the wind. But yes, once he's back on dry land we'll I'll go out for dinner. Sound like a plan?"

"Sounds like a plan, boss. Look for those contracts in the next ten or fifteen minutes. Tell your parents I said hi."

"Will do and as always, Diana, thank you for everything you do. I really appreciate you."

"Yeah, yeah, yeah. Appreciate me in my next bonus. Goodbye, loverboy."

As the laundry finished, rather than putting it away, right back in the luggage it went. I glanced around my condo seeing it through fresh eyes. Bland, boring, stale. How had I never bothered to decorate before or really turn it into a home? It was as though I had one foot out the door the entire time I'd lived here. Should I bother to decorate now? Make it more comfortable for when Vale came over? Though in reality I couldn't picture us here long-term. Hell, at this point I hardly pictured myself here.

Vale and I here?

Wow, how far ahead of our new relationship could I get?

There was no denying the thoughts I'd had of us in a house where he could monkey around, for lack of a better descriptive. What would it take to build an indoor gym with a rock wall? Maybe those metal bars we had in grade school that you swung along on. I could see him swinging from handle to handle. Actually, that would be a great piece of workout equipment for both of us.

The wheels turned at an alarming rate.

With those thoughts fresh in my mind, I booted up my laptop, poured a glass of wine and dove into a new home search. There had to be houses around here with gyms already in them for sale. Or ones with the space to add a gym. Having any outdoors would diminish usage to three months of the year here. Seattle rain and all of that. My condo had a great view of Lake Washington, which was the reason I purchased it, but now I wanted a place for two. How was it I spent my life in and out of dating, never once had I envisioned a future with another yet now that was all that I saw?

Life without Vale wasn't an option for me, and I'd do whatever it took to ensure his happiness.

I loved my parents' place on Whidbey. Five acres of land. A gorgeous two-story, thirty-five-hundred square foot house. Five bedrooms, three bathrooms. Way too big for them, though they did love to entertain and it was nice that I had my own room there. I wondered what Vale would think of living on the island. That idea opened a secondary home search, one for north of Seattle and up to Anacortes, and now another for Whidbey.

Maybe it would be best to buy land and build the house of our dreams.

That night as I lay awake in bed, unable to shut my brain down, I shot off a text to Vale.

Me: *I hope you're doing okay.*

Cheesy? Maybe...

I tossed and turned all night, well aware it could be hours if not days before I'd hear back from him. He had the job from hell, really, and ran nonstop. Finally, I dozed off and when I woke the first thing I did was reach for my phone.

Vale: *Sorry it took so long to get back to you. Today has been miserable. We worked sixteen hours then when we got back to the room we both passed out. How was your day? You're probably sleeping. I hope I didn't wake you. Love you!*

My sweet, thoughtful boy. It'd only been twenty-four hours since I last saw him, and I missed his rambling.

Me: *My day was boring. Today I'm going to visit my parents and stay for a few days. Love you too, Monkey.*

After a quick shower, I grabbed my bag, hit my favorite coffee shop and was on my way to catch the ferry out of Mukilteo. Once boarded, I went above deck and snagged a window seat and took a couple of pictures for Vale. I loved gazing out at the Sound every time I rode the ferries. The views of the islands were amazing. I loved living here. Washington was a gorgeous state with so much to offer between fishing, outdoor activities, wine tasting—the options to fill one's time were never ending. As soon as I sat, Vale texted back.

Vale: *I love the pictures. So pretty. I've only been to Whidbey once and I loved it. We went to this red barn place. I remember there was a swing set outside I played on while my mom shopped.*

Me: *Yes. I always stop on the way to my parents' and pick up wine and cheese there. I've often thought of having a home on the island.*

Thought I'd throw that out there and get his thoughts on it.

> Vale: *That would be amazing but so far for me to come and see you.*

> Me: *That's a minor detail that's easily remedied.*

I bet my parents would love having Vale's mother around. Probably a good idea to bring her out and meet them first. Maybe at the same time I brought Vale. There was plenty of room at my parents' house for a weekend meet and greet and we could take them to all our favorite places.

Then I could spring the whole moving to the island proposal to Vale.

Proposal...

Did that word just enter my head?

Talk about a whirlwind romance. *Slow your roll, Jack.*

A true mirrored image of my father I was.

Maybe a mother-in-law suite could be added to the plans. Good God, was I getting ahead of myself. *Jack, you've lost your fucking mind.* Mother-in-law suites, houses with property.

I shook my head and laughed. Anyone near me had to think I was insane right now. They couldn't hear my thoughts, but they could see my reactions. Yet I couldn't shake any of them because they felt so right. Like, bone deep rightness. Vail and I haven't even really dated, and I was already so far gone there were no reins to stop my forward motion by.

The familiar red barn came into view. I pulled in and parked and snapped a picture as I walked up to it, then sent it off to Vale, he'd get a kick out of that. I perused the wine and cheese and made a few selections to share with my parents. As soon as I drove up to their house, Mom came running out of the front door.

"There's my baby boy!" Though I towered over her, it still felt wonderful to be in her arms as she wrapped them around me in a mother's loving embrace. "Let me help you with the groceries." She grabbed the bags from the backseat while my father hugged me and helped with the luggage.

"Jeez, son, how long were you planning to stay for? Or did you decide to move back in?"

My parents were wonderful, and their home was always open to me.

"Ha-ha-ha. Nice try, but no. I know how much Mom would love to cook for me again but everything's fine, trust me."

"That's because you don't eat enough, and you don't eat well. And a mother knows best," she fired off. Dad and I shared a knowing glance that said we were both smart enough to keep our mouths shut and not argue with the lady in charge.

"Just wanted to get away and clear my head. Nothing wrong with that, is there?"

"Not unless it has something to do with a certain mister your mother told me about?"

"Maybe."

Mom had lunch ready and waiting on the dining table. The three of us got caught up while we ate just like old times. How long had it been since my last visit? Far too long and I made a mental note to not go this far between visits again. Vale, of course, was the topic of discussion, and I shared all but the intimate details. Those were meant for us and us alone, memories to reflect upon in private.

"I just knew the moment I met him that he was the one." Instalove, soulmates, whatever you called it, Vale was that and more for me.

"Typical Barrett reaction." Mom smiled across the table at Dad. To think I finally had a chance at what they have had for nearly forty years of marriage was mind boggling. They still looked at each other like the sun rose and set within them.

Beautiful. There was no other way to describe it.

"This is true, son," Dad readily agreed. "We Barretts just know. But remember, those which our hearts want and are enamored with may get spooked by our forwardness. Do you think your young man will be able to handle a Barrett coming at him full force?"

I sat back and blew out a deep breath as I pondered his question. "I hope so. Vale seemed more concerned with whether I'd be able to handle him."

"Why is that?" Mom chimed in.

"He's neurodiverse, ADHD—heavy on the H if you get my drift. He's been rejected by others because he was too much for them. Whereas for me he is the opposite. You know how much I enjoy having a boy, whether it be a little or a pet, though I usually prefer pets. Well, I actually helped him embrace and accept his inner pet. I watched him from afar the first time he entered the playroom on the ship, completely enthralled with what he saw. The next time he appeared it was in a makeshift monkey costume he'd thrown together. The most horrendous thing I'd ever seen." I smiled at the recollection and my parents laughed. "Yet it called to him, his inner monkey. It was utterly perfect. Once he found pet play it was the perfect outlet for his energy and everything just clicked into place."

"Of course, you've already purchased him a new suit, I'd imagine?" Dad knowingly winked.

"Absolutely. It's sitting on my dining table waiting for him to open it. I think he'll enjoy the club and all it has to offer." At least I hoped he did.

"Why do I have a feeling you've got a few more plans up your sleeve for your monkey?" Mom's bright smile only served to widen mine.

"Because I'm your son and you know me well." I'd argue to say too well, though the connection I had with my parents ran deep and I wouldn't change it for anything.

"Come on, son. Let's go out on the deck and enjoy a cocktail." Dad rose and we helped clear the dishes before I stepped outside.

He'd get no argument from me. Dad only stocked the best bourbon and libations. All of which he purchased from local island distilleries.

Outside on my parents' balcony, the temperature was great, and they had a perfect view of the sound. As I took it in, wishing Vale was by my side, I wondered where in the world he was today.

"What's going on in that handsome head of yours?" Dad asked as he handed me a glass and clinked his against mine.

"Handsome, huh? I look just like you."

"That's how I know you're handsome. All right, my boy, talk to me."

"Dad, I'm head over heels in love with him."

"I suspected as much. Does he feel the same way?"

"He says he does, but once he's on land again, what if that changes?" Fuck, that would break me.

Chapter Eleven
Jack

"Daddy!" Vale giggled as his face filled the computer screen. "It's been far too long since I got to see you."

"Same, Sweet Monkey. How's the cruise?" We'd texted the last couple of days, but Vale hadn't had time for a facetime call let alone a computer video chat.

"Boring and busy. It's not a kink cruise this time so instead of taking a break for me at the end of the night to play, I just keep going until my limbs can't move anymore." He sighed. "I miss monkey."

"I'm sorry, love. As soon as you get back I'll schedule a play date at the club for you." Poor guy was probably stressed beyond anything.

"Really? That would be fun. Do you think the other pets will like me? Maybe they'll play with me? I hope they don't make fun of my homemade costume."

"Don't worry about that, sweetheart." I nearly slipped and gave away his surprise.

"Oh, I almost forgot." He nervously fidgeted. "I told my mom about you."

"Good, 'cause I told mine, too."

Sharing with his mom was a good sign he was serious about us.

"She, um..." he trailed off.

"Spit it out, Little Monkey. I promise I won't get mad."

"She's insisting you come to dinner after you meet me at the docks."

I'd expected nothing less from a mom as caring as Vale's. "Absolutely, not a problem."

"Whew." Vale visibly relaxed.

"What were you afraid of?" Hopefully not me.

"That you'd call it off. Not want to be with someone who's as close to their mother as I am. Momma's boy, I've been called."

"Then I'm one, too. I'm still here at my parents' place, thoroughly enjoying our time together."

"Momma's boys are the best!" my mom shouted from behind me.

"See what I mean?"

"Jackson, give me the phone. I want to see that beau of yours."

"Beau? Really, Mom?" She tapped my shoulder in a mock slap, and I handed the phone over.

"There you are. What a cutie. Hello, Vale, I'm Linda, Jackson's mother. It's so nice to see you. I can't wait until Jackson brings you out to visit us."

Poor Vale's face went a dangerous shade of red.

"Um, hi?" He waved at the phone, so freaking cute. "It's nice to meet you, Mrs. Barrett."

"There'll be none of that Mrs. nonsense. Please, call me Linda."

"And I'm Jackson Senior." Dad waved from behind us. My poor boy didn't know what to do.

"I think the screen is frozen, Jack, his face hasn't moved."

"No, it's not frozen, but you've scared the hell out of him."

"Oh, sweetheart, I didn't mean to do that. We're really nice, I swear," Mom pleaded with Vale who finally smiled.

"Sorry, I've never met anyone's parents before besides Darcy. She's my best friend." Just then her cherub face appeared.

"Hi everyone!" She waved at the screen. "I love that you embarrassed Vale."

"Shut up, Darcy," Vale tried and failed to whisper.

"I'm gonna tell your Daddy on you," she retorted, and I choked back a laugh.

"Heard him loud and clear. That's not too nice, Little Monkey."

"Oh my God. Your parents are hearing all of this." His head hit the top of the desk. "Mortified." Darcy was behind him dancing with laughter and I nearly did the same. My parents were more than aware of my lifestyle and had no problems with it.

"No need for that, Vale. We know about our son's kinks."

"Did your mother just use the word kink?" That only seemed to draw Vale further down. "Could the ground, or the sea please swallow me whole?"

Poor guy, everyone but Vale was laughing now.

"Here," Mom handed the phone back. "I think you need to talk your boy off the ledge."

Once everyone on both sides of the call wandered off and left Vale and I alone, I walked down to the shore and flipped the camera around. "Look at this gorgeous view. So relaxing. I can't wait to share it with you."

Another sigh. "Me, too, Daddy. Do your parents really know about us and the pet stuff?"

"They do and they know about littles and bit about other kinks, too. They're no shamers. They're good, down to earth people. You'll love them. Fair warning, though, my mother loves to cook and insists we all need to eat more." That got a smile. "There's my gorgeous boy."

"I miss you so much. Thankfully I have a different cabin assignment this trip. I just don't think I could clean your cabin for someone else."

"My heart aches without you near, sweet boy. Just a few more weeks until we'll be together again but know that I'm gonna have a hard time being away from you after that." That was putting it mildly, but I didn't want to come across stalkerish.

"I hope so because I plan to become that an-noying pest that never leaves his Daddy's side."

"I look forward to it."

"Shoot. I have to go. I love you."

"I love you, too, Monkey."

Being the Daddy wasn't always easy. Take for instance, having to let my boy go when all I wanted to do was send a helicopter to pick him up and bring him to me.

"Does my boy need a warm brownie and a glass of milk?"

"Mom, while I will always be your boy, I'm past the age of milk." Was I really, though?

Because that combination sounded damn good, and the knowing glance Mom gave said she knew that, too. "You win. Yes, please and thank you."

It did pay to come home every once in a while, if only to get a bit spoiled.

"I like your friend, Jack," Mom said, as she set a plate with a warm brownie and a scoop of vanilla ice cream in front of me while Dad poured us each a glass of milk. "He seems sweet and very young."

"Linda, you know our boy has a penchant for them in a certain age range. Not that there's a problem with that. Vale's a bit timid. Handsome young fellow, though."

"From everything he's told me, he hasn't had it very easy dating wise. I mean, I know people have had an issue with his energy, but men have really treated him like shit, to be honest, which I'll never understand. Vale's sweet, kind, adorable and I had so much fun watching him find himself and just be free. But what the others missed, I found so honestly, I should be thanking them, though if I ever run into one of them, thanking them isn't exactly what I'd do.

But I'm the lucky one here, the one that gets to be with him." Wow, I can't believe I let all that out. The thoughts had been in my head but not necessarily meant to be shared.

"And that, Jack, is one of the sweetest accolades I've ever heard." Mom kissed the top on my head as she sat down. It was like I was ten all over again. "You have a heart of gold, my boy, and I'm glad you finally found someone to treat you with the respect you deserve."

My gaze set on the water through the sliding glass door. "It's so beautiful here. It's like once you drive off the ferry you're in a whole other world, one where you've left your troubles behind. I'm never more relaxed than I am when I'm here."

"You know, the land next door is for sale. Have you ever thought of building a home?" My head whipped toward my father so fast I feared I'd throw my neck out. "I was just saying, son, no need to get your hackles up."

"Quite the opposite, Dad. I've been thinking about buying land and building a house on it." But would having my parents as neighbors be good or bad? Definitely something to consider.

After the heavy snack, I took a walk down along the water. Just me and my thoughts. Ironically enough, my feet led the way while my mind wandered and when I stopped I faced the sale sign for the lot and snapped a picture of it. Once I was home I'd think long and hard about my options. It wasn't like I was in any rush. But by the same token, I wasn't in love with where I was at, residence wise.

A chill filled the air as the sun began its descent and I returned to my parents' house. Mom was at the stove starting dinner and Dad was in front of the TV watching a documentary. On what I had no clue, but I took a seat on the couch next to his recliner.

"I guess we're not barbequing."

"Didn't have any steaks. Are you all right, son?"

"Yeah, I'm just struggling a bit with this rush of emotions. It's overwhelming. I mean, I'm moving at an unstoppable pace and desire things that generally don't come until a year or two into a relationship. It's like I'm trying to cram ten years' worth of getting to know somebody and everything associated with that into a few weeks. I looked at the land next door, and I'm not gonna lie, I would absolutely love to buy it and build a house there. But I don't want to freak Vale out." Fuck, what was wrong with me? "I'm moving too fast."

"Understandable. It might feel fast now, but by the time he gets back you'll have maintained a long-distance relationship for a few months. And from the sounds of it, he's all in. They always say absence makes the heart grow fonder and in this case, that might work in your favor. Only you and Vale can determine if you're moving too fast. Not a calendar. Not society. Not anyone outside of the two of you."

I hadn't thought of it that way. Each day apart grew increasingly harder for me and if it was the same way for him, he may never want to be apart either. Vale was his own man. He made his own decisions, and he was the one to ultimately decide what he wanted to do. All I could do was make the offer and share my dreams and see if Vale's aligned or if we could find a suitable compromise.

After dinner, my parents met some friends for drinks. While they asked me to come, I decided I'd rather not. My mood wasn't the best and bringing their evening down I'd never do. I spent a few more days at their house, having only heard from Vale via phone once and the rest of the time by text. I wished every call would be facetime so I could see him, but I understood that wasn't always possible. Though the simple *I'm thinking of you, Daddy* and *I love you* texts would carry me through until we were together again.

Everything returned to normal, or how it was pre–Vale, as soon as I got home. Going into the office daily I quickly learned was a waste of time, but I had nowhere else to be and I hated being alone now. With Diana in charge, there were no worries, which only intensified the desire to live on the island. Rarely would I need to be in the office and if I did Vale and I could make a trip of it and spend a few days in the city, get a hotel and live it up and play at Blush.

"What happened to the happy Jack that I talked to when he got back from his cruise? All we're getting now is mopey Jack, and you're bringing morale down," Diana teased, though there was truth in her words.

"I miss him. The house is too empty, too quiet. He calls when he can, and I understand his job comes first but what the brain understands, the heart does not." Would those two organs ever live in peace and harmony?

"When my husband was stationed overseas, had the kids and I not stayed with family I would have been lost and overwhelmed, to be honest. It's a lot to raise two kids on your own and even more so when you don't hear from your spouse or significant other for months on end. When he deployed there were times he wasn't allowed to contact us and all I knew was that he was out there fighting for our country and putting his life on the line and there was nothing I could do. Now while Vale isn't in the military and it's not exactly the same, I do understand the heart and the brain not communicating or being on the same page."

Now I felt like a whiney baby. "I'm glad everything worked out fine and your husband came home." Diana had shared with me in the past about the PTSD her husband suffered from since retiring from the military and returning home. I couldn't imagine what our soldiers went through. Just thanking them for their service would never be enough. Not only did they put their lives on their line, but their minds never forgot the horrific things they witnessed.

"Doesn't Vale get back soon?"

"Yes, as a matter of fact, it's next week." Not that I was counting the days, or the hours...

"And you're taking time off, correct?" She gave me that warning eye, the one that said if I hadn't planned to she'd make sure I did.

"As well as can be expected of me but you know I'll still be available to you."

"I do, but make sure you put him first. Show him the true Jackson Barrett, the wonderful man that I've worked with for over a decade and wouldn't have it any other way. You've got a heart of gold, Jack, and if Vale isn't head over heels for you already, he soon will be."

"I don't think I pay you enough, Diana."

She laughed. "You pay me well, but I'd never say no to a raise. Now go on, get out of here and get everything ready for when your boy comes home."

Home.

I was so ready to have that with Vale.

I took her advice and spent the next few days getting the condo in order, ensuring groceries were stocked and the place was clean even though my cleaning lady made sure it was. Of course, I did far too much shopping. The dining table was covered in packages waiting for my boy to unwrap them. The night before his return, I hardly slept.

Far too excited, I arrived at the docks too early, even though I knew the staff were the last ones to disembark. But when I saw his face appear in the crowd it made the long, excruciating wait more than worth it. Long gone and far behind us were the late-night chats that had become few and far between.

No more.

I had my boy back.

Chapter Twelve
Vale

"Daddy!" I squealed and ran straight into Jack's open arms. Happy tears ran free, and I had no desire to stop them. I had my Daddy back, and I was one excited boy and he was trapped, ha-ha, having Ubered up to meet me and left his car at home.

"Sweet Monkey, I missed you terribly." Daddy peppered my face in kisses. "The backpack fits you perfectly." So glad I decided to wear it today. It was fun and fashionable and held my stuffies from Daddy perfectly so they were always with me.

"Ahem," Darcy cleared her throat beside us. "I'm down for a good show but are you guys sure this is the time and place?"

"Smart ass," I nudged her with my shoulder. "Let's get our luggage and go home."

Daddy held my hand all the way to the carousel, and I nearly skipped a couple of times along the way but managed to refrain. "Are you nervous about dinner?"

"No, should I be?" Daddy eyed me curiously, waiting for a punch line or something.

"Vale's mom is super sweet, you're gonna love her. She's like a second mom to me," Darcy happily shared.

"Will you be joining us tonight, Darcy?" Daddy asked her. Always including Darcy. I loved it and she did, too.

"Probably. My mom will likely be working."

"Yes, she will be." I hated that when Darcy was home she was always alone. I got it, her mom worked two jobs, but she had for as long as I'd known Darcy. Their finances were of no concern of mine, but my friend's wellbeing was.

"Okay, yes, looks like I'll be there." She grinned wide. Apparently Darcy listened to Daddy more than me.

"Yay!" I cheered, beyond excited to spend the first day at home surrounded by everyone I loved.

Daddy laughed. "Excellent. As Vale's best friend, I look forward to getting to know you better."

Swoon. Swoon. Daddy held my heart in the palm of his hand and was determined to win Darcy over. Little did he know he already had. Could he be any more perfect?

It's funny how easily I fell into calling him Daddy. At first I was like, no way, but the more he catered to and cared for me the more natural it became. Now I'd have a hard time remembering to use his real name when in group settings or around our families.

"Vale," Darcy slammed the car trunk shut. "How many times have we had this conversation?"

I knew exactly where this was headed. "In my defense, I didn't know I'd not only have a boyfriend but that he'd be joining us, or I'd have cleaned the car first."

"Lies! All Lies!" Darcy hollered as she hopped in the back seat.

Grr. I hated it when she was right.

"Sweet boy," Daddy grabbed the fast-food bag off the passenger seat and placed it in the near-by trashcan. "Do you live in your car?"

"Kind of?"

"Wait, what if your car doesn't start? It's been parked here for four months." Daddy was a worrywart.

"We leave the keys with them, and they start them once a week for us." I buckled up and put the car in gear. Traffic to get out of the parking garage was horrendous and didn't let up until I'd passed Northgate on our way to Lynnwood where Darcy and I lived. The closer we got to home, the tighter my stomach got.

Jack rubbed my thigh. "Are you okay, Vale?"

"Yes. No. Maybe."

"Too late to wonder, here comes your mom," Darcy announced and promptly hopped out to hug my mom.

"Here goes nothing." Jack and I walked toward Mom, her eyes assessing him all the way. "Hi, Mom." She yanked me to her and eyed me from head to toe, looking for...water damage? Could a human grow mold? No clue but when she was satisfied she hugged me.

"You look good, Vale, and your man is handsome, but is he worthy?" Wow, Mom didn't even use her whisper voice.

Oh shit, here we go.

"Jackson Barrett." Jack extended his hand. "Nice to meet you, Mrs. Harper."

Mom paused, a moment too long if you asked me, before she returned the gesture. "Please, call me Sarah."

"Wonderful to meet you, Sarah. Vale has told me many wonderful things about you."

"He's got it in his head he gets some sort of trust fund when I die so he thinks he gets paid to say nice things."

"Mom!" Darcy nearly doubled over laughing and I was beyond stunned at her brazen behavior. "Woman, what has gotten into you?" Likely the devil, though I'd not say that aloud. She'd probably put laxatives in my food if I did.

"You're right, Darcy, I do like her." Jack winked at me. "Why don't you and Darcy go inside, and I'll get the luggage. Darcy, should I bring yours in as well?"

"We can help you, Daddy." Fuck. Fuck. Fuckity fuck. It was like time halted and the entire world tuned in to watch the war that was about to unfold.

"Daddy?" Mom questioned. "He's not your father and if he was this would be one sick ass stunt, son."

"No, not like that kind of Daddy, but like a handler Daddy." Shit, that wasn't any better. Before I could explain, she kicked into protective mother bear mode.

"Handler? You think my boy needs a handler? He's perfect the way he is and has never required being handled before. If you think that way you best move along, Jackson." Mom was pissed.

Fuck. My. Life.

"I agree," Jack stepped in. "Vale is perfect the way he is and doesn't need a handler. One of many reasons why I prefer to be called Daddy, and not in the blood relative sense but in the boyfriend way. I care deeply for your son, I'm in love with him and it's in my nature to take care of those I love."

"I think this conversation is best had inside, Jackson," Mom flipped off our nosy neighbor. Jack didn't know what to say but Darcy was back to laughing. "Nosy woman next door is all up in our business."

The way this woman talked. Where did she get it from?

"Mom, we need to limit your reality TV time. Flipping off the neighbors is not wise."

"Wise my ass. I'd like to see her old ass try and get a piece of me."

I had nowhere to run. Nowhere to hide, though I did consider going for a long jog off a short and hopefully nearby cliff.

Mom stepped back inside while the three of us grabbed the luggage. "Jack, I'm so sorry. I should've warned you she's a loose cannon. Especially when it comes to me."

"Good, I'm glad. Makes me like her even more. Lots of energy and fiercely protective. Love it."

Could I hide now? Those two teaming up would be a scary thing.

Jack sat Darcy's luggage just inside the door while I took mine to my room and hadn't realized he'd followed me until his arms wrapped around my waist from behind and he whispered, "Deep breath, Monkey. Everything will be fine."

"I hope so. This wasn't the impression I wanted to make. Thank God she doesn't own a gun or she'd have been on the front porch waving it around." That image would haunt me for the rest of my life. "We're not even from the south, both born and raised here yet she just came off like a *Beverly Hillbillies* rerun." Mom and I spent many nights binging series from her childhood, though this was the first time I'd come to regret it.

Jack's chuckle rumbled through me. "She did and it was adorable."

"You say that now, but just wait." No clue what had gotten into that woman, but I was about to call bullshit on her crazy ass antics.

"Hey, Vale, pack an overnight bag." Daddy winked and my face heated. I knew what that meant and I was so pent up I was near bursting. Which would be bad. Oh my god, what if I came too soon? There went my brain... "Deep breath, Vale."

Daddy knew me too well. I nodded and shoved a few things into my new backpack and set it on top of Darcy's bags in the entryway.

"Boys, come on out. Don't be getting into none of that freaky shit." Mom's voice echoed down the hall.

"Just kill me now."

Daddy kissed the top of my head. "Not a chance, baby."

"Have a seat, Jackson. Tell me how you and my son came together."

Every time she opened her mouth, it only got worse.

"I'd say spare no details but there are some things a mother doesn't need to know." She rolled her eyes at herself. Who did that?

"Really? Now you're drawing boundaries." The audacity of this woman. "You're talking like a hillbilly thug, neither of which you are. What have you been watching while I was gone?"

"None ya," she smugly replied.

"None ya?"

"Yeah, none ya business."

"OMG, I'm shutting off the cable."

"You'll do no such thing. Now, unbunch your panties and come sit by your beau."

"Best. Night. Ever," Darcy announced from her perch at the end of the couch. All she was missing was a bucket of popcorn, watching the show like it was a televised event.

"Only because you're not in the hot seat." Pouting would get me nowhere and I needed to schedule my mother for a lobotomy.

"Little Monkey, come here." Daddy patted his lap, and I curled up on it. With my head resting above his heart, mine calmed down. "She's just trying to understand our relationship and get to know me."

"And poking fun at my expense and thoroughly embarrassing me."

"Jeez, Vale, can't a mother have a little fun?" Finally, Mom's normal voice returned.

"You're a kindergarten teacher who just came off as a Louisville thug."

"Now look who's got jokes." And back to the attitude-filled southern drawl.

"Oh my god, I don't even know what to do with you." My head shook as Daddy's chest rumbled with laughter.

"Sweet boy, she's just messing around." Daddy brushed the hair out of my eyes. "Please, Sarah, I know you have many questions and outside of personal ones such as our sex life, I'm an open book so ask away."

"Explain to me why my son mentioned you're a handler. Is that like training people to be something or someone they're not?"

"No. I live a kink lifestyle. I've had boys who are littles and middles." Darcy's intense stare was on me, I winked to let her know her secret was safe. This was about Vale and me, not her, and if she wanted to share that was her prerogative. "And I've had pups before. Those dynamics are considered a kink. On this trip I suggested to Vale he look into pet play as a means to release excess energy. I have zero problems with Vale or his neurodiversity, but he was concerned I would. In his research he decided to try pet play and on his own found his inner monkey."

"Inner monkey?"

"Yes. Pet play, littles, BDSM, praise, impact play—those and many more are forms of release. Outlets. To some therapy while to others a means to do nothing more than get off. When a person gets into any one of those mindsets, or subspaces as they're called, they find a way to release what plagues them, rest their minds, or in Vale's case, a way to release excess energy and tire himself out."

"Did it work?" Ah, now she was curious.

"Better than anything else has, Mom. Sometimes my brain just won't shut off but on the nights I got to play before bed I was far more relaxed, and it slowed it down enough for me to sleep. Some nights I got five to six hours versus the normal three to four. Daddy, err, Jack is going to take me to the club here so I can check it out and play with others like me there."

"I'm not going to pretend I understand it and I will be researching it myself. You're holding precious cargo right know, Jackson. That boy is my world and I'll protect him with my life until the day I die."

"As will I, Sarah. I have fallen head over heels in love with your son and would like to build a life with him, if he'll have me, that is." Daddy's confession blew me away. We'd spoken, albeit briefly, about these things and I just thought they were chatty talk. A way to fill our conversations, but now I knew Daddy meant it.

"Oh, Daddy!" Again, with happy tears, but I couldn't help it and even if I could I'm not sure I would have. "I love you so much."

"All right." Mom slapped her hands together. "Who wants pizza?"

"Please, Sarah, allow me." Daddy slid his phone from his pocket. "What does everyone like on theirs?"

I followed Mom to the kitchen and left Darcy and Daddy in the living room chatting while Daddy ordered dinner. "Mom, what gives?"

"What do you mean, Vale?"

"The attitude, the failed attempt at using slang? Seriously, no more reality TV."

She laughed. "I was just messing with you and Jackson. He seems like a nice guy. A bit old for you, though, don't you think?"

Ah, now we were getting somewhere. "Honestly, no. The guys my age have treated me like a piece of meat. Jack has been the perfect gentleman, always looking out for me and making sure I'm taking care of myself and getting enough sleep. He's everything I ever hoped for and more."

"I see that in him. The way he looks at you and had zero concern about holding you in front of me. He knew what you needed, and he put that need first." She pulled the plates and napkins out. "I just don't want you to get hurt."

"Mom, I've already been hurt which is why I had barely left the house before I took this job. Jack won't hurt me. I believe that with every ounce of my being." I did. There wasn't a single red flag with Jack. Not yet at least and the really ugly ones usually showed themselves pretty quickly.

"Sorry, Vale, I didn't know."

"That's on me. I didn't want to tell you. I felt like such a fool each time and it hurt like hell, Mom. That was more than embarrassing than your hillbilly gangster routine tonight." I wish I could've filmed it and played it back for her later. She'd have lost her shit.

Instead, she laughed. "It was all in good fun, Vale. But I'm glad you're home safe and sound."

"Me, too, Mom. Me, too."

"Wow." The food came and the boxes never ended. "How many people were you planning to feed?"

Daddy smiled and shut the door. "Well, everyone wanted something different so we each got our own pizza. But the salad, wings, and breadsticks were tempting so I ordered those, too."

Was it possible to feel something more than hard, soul-deep love for another human?

As the evening wound down and Mom had run out of questions, thank fuck for that, it was time to call it a night.

"Sarah, it was wonderful to meet you. You have a lovely home, and a wonderful son." Daddy had a way with words and making me blush.

"Yes, I do and I'm trusting you to take care of him."

"That's a promise I can make and will keep." Daddy turned to Darcy. "Can we drop you off at home?"

"Yes, please."

"Okay, I'll load your stuff up while you guys say your goodbyes. Thank you again, Sarah. We'll get together soon. I'd like you to meet my parents."

I handed Daddy the keys to my car and he took Darcy's stuff out.

"Meet his parents? This sounds serious, Vale." Mom was concerned and I got it, having had the same reaction when he mentioned me meeting them.

"It is, but it feels right. Does that make sense?"

"It does, baby boy. I'd say be careful, but something tells me Jackson, or Jack, not sure which to call him, is the one."

"Me, too, Mom." We hugged and said goodbye and Darcy and I met Jack at the car, who'd made himself at home in the driver's seat.

"Where to, Darcy?" our new chauffeur asked as Darcy gave him directions to her house.

We pulled up to it ten minutes later. Pitch black inside and her mom's car, which they both shared, was gone.

"Darcy, let us help you inside," Daddy insisted. Protective of me, protective of Darcy. Daddy was the real deal in Daddy land.

Chapter Thirteen
Jack

We pulled into the underground parking beneath my building, and I parked in the open space that was also mine beside my car. A sudden rush of nerves hit me. Other boys had been here, I was no saint, but this time was different. The desire to impress Vale, for him to be comfortable in my home was heightened. A place I hoped to share together while we built one specifically tailored for us.

Us.

How easily that simple word rolled off my tongue and now here we were, finally together again. Silently we rode the elevator up and it felt like this was the first time I'd done this, having another in my private space. I guess in essence it was with Vale. The first and hopefully the last man I'd bring home and the only one whose opinion mattered to me.

"Wow." Vale gasped as we stepped inside and headed straight for the wall of windows that looked out over Lake Washington. I'd made sure to leave the curtains open when I left this morning so his eyes would immediately go to it. "This view is incredible."

"It's the whole reason I bought this place." I sat his bag down and tossed his keys in the bowl on the entry table. "But I must say, the view is a whole lot better with you in it."

"Daddy, you say the sweetest things."

I slid my arms around his waist and nuzzled his neck. "Feels like I've waited a lifetime to have you here."

"Your whiskers tickle, Daddy." A sweet giggle escaped. "Why don't you give me the grand tour?"

"Okay, let's start in the dining area." My place was an open concept layout with the common areas as one and the dining table was visible from where we were. "First thing I did when I bought this place was take down the walls that blocked the view."

"Is it somebody's birthday?" Vale eyed the stacks of gifts.

"Those are for you, Monkey."

"Me?" His eyes lit up as he took the pile in. "All of them?"

"Yes, all of them. Have at it." He ripped into them with all the vigor of a kid on Christmas morning and I got lost in his excitement.

"Daddy! Daddy! Daddy!" He yanked the new monkey suit from the box. "Is this what I think it is? A suit of my own? A real one to wear to Blush?"

"Yes, sweet boy, that's exactly what it is. Not that there was anything wrong with the one you made, but this one will fit a bit better." I felt the need to clarify, upsetting or offending my boy wasn't going to happen on my watch.

"This is wonderful. The other one was itchy."

Thank fuck. Until he opened it I hadn't realized how horribly wrong this could've gone.

"Mine all mine," he sang as held it against his chest and spun around.

"There's more."

Next one he unwrapped was the external tail attached to a belt. As he reached for the one I knew held the internal tail, I held my breath in anticipation of his reaction.

"Oh my." Red-faced, he stared down at the silver plug. "I've, um, I've never worn a plug before."

This just got very interesting...

"Would you like to try it tonight?"

"Just the tail?"

"Yes, just the tail."

"'Kay."

He finished unwrapping the rest, a koala stuffie and a crop top that said "Daddy's Monkey" on the front of it.

"Come on, I'll show you the rest of the place." We went through the living room, which he'd already seen, then he peeked into the guest room, laundry room which was in the hallway, guest bath, and then lastly, the main bedroom and bath.

"So, this is your bedroom?"

Hmm, did I detect a hint of nerves in my boy or was it something else?

"Yes. Vale, nothing will happen that you don't want to. I'm perfectly happy to spend our first night together cuddling and talking the night away, peacefully content. I'm just happy you're here. Zero expectations, I just want to hold my boy and have him fall asleep in my arms."

"What if I want something more to happen?"

"Such as?" Assumptions were not the right way to go, Vale's intentions must be clear.

Vale flirtingly ran the end of the plug over my chest. "How about we shower, together, and then we see how well this fits?" He waved the plug around.

"Sassy, sassy, naughty boy. I like how you think." And so did my dick as it sprang to life.

Slowly he worked the buttons on my shirt open and held onto his tail the entire time like a lifeline. "I missed you, Daddy." Vale trailed kisses up my chest, I met him halfway and pressed my mouth to his.

"I've missed these lips."

"Is that all you've missed, Daddy?'

With a firm grip on his ass, I tugged him tightly to me and rubbed my erection against his. "Not even close."

Lips slightly parted, Vale accepted the invitation and slid his tongue along mine as they tangled in a familiar dance. Everything about this boy called to me, drove me crazy. He was all I'd ever wanted but didn't know I'd need. I wanted to breathe the air he breathed, bask in his scent, enjoy every moment of life we had together.

Silently, we finished undressing, sneaking peeks and shy glances along the way. Fun and flirty, what an enlightening way to spend this pivotal moment in our relationship. So much for a sexy shower first, being inside my boy was best served first.

"Lie back, Little Monkey, and let Daddy worship you the way you were meant to be." His slight blush at my words only served to fuel my desire to show my boy how special he was. Inch by salacious inch.

Lips, hands, fingers, every part of me I had control over touched Vale. Skin smooth as silk, so young and beautiful. I nuzzled his curls nestled around his cock and inhaled deeply, gazing up at the wonderful man who entrusted me with his body. How had others missed what a gift this was? To be allowed to worship this perfect being?

I was one lucky man.

"Spread your legs, my love." The gentle command came out in an unsteady voice. My mind was a whirlwind of everything I wished to pleasure my boy with. I had to pull back my own reins and reel in the gaggle of emotions that flowed through me.

Save some for later, Jack. There'll be plenty of time...

He spread his legs and I positioned between them and licked a strip up his shaft, around the head and back down.

"Daddy," he moaned.

"Yes, sweet boy, Daddy will take care of you."

"Promise?

Still so unsure.

"Always, my love. Daddy will always take care of his boy."

Lower I licked, savoring every gasp and moan elicited like fuel to the fire that burned inside me. Farther down I edged along his perineum to his precious hole. A single swipe of tongue and my boy arched up.

"Oh my god, do that again. Please."

Had no one ever done this for him?

I licked and sucked and nibbled until my boy relaxed enough for my tongue to slide inside. He writhed and moaned and recited an unfamiliar, barely audible chant.

"Daddy, Daddy. Gonna, gonna..."

Firmly I gripped the base of his cock. "Not until Daddy's inside you, sweet boy. Is that what you want? To feel Daddy's cock throb inside you as we come?"

"God. Yes. Please. Now."

Yes, full sentences were not going to happen and given that the condom versus no condom conversation hadn't been had, now was not the time for it. We both needed to be of sound mind when we had it and both were perched atop that precarious edge. Next time there would be no barrier. Just Vale and me as I came inside his tight channel and filled him with my come and marked him as mine. Not that he already wasn't, but that act was one I'd never performed with another.

Vale protested when I moved to gather the supplies from the nightstand. "Sorry, sweet boy, I'll just be a moment." I suited up, applied lube and worked him further open. Hurting my boy would never happen.

"Daddy, I'm ready. Please."

That tiny plea nearly undid me. Vale drew his knees up and held his legs wide open as I pressed the head of cock to his entrance. *Easy, Jack, take your time. He's more than worth it.*

Did other men talk themselves off come-induced ledges or was I an anomaly?

"More," Vale moaned and gripped my hips.

"Sweet boy, Daddy doesn't want to hurt you." I wasn't sure how long it had been for him, and I wasn't about to go balls deep on the first thrust.

"No hurt. Need Daddy."

Fucking hell. Everything that came out of my boy's mouth was like an aphrodisiac.

Once I was fully seated inside him, I took a moment for both of us. If I didn't get a grip this would be over far too soon. So tight, the perfect tension surrounded my cock, like a warm embrace.

Perfect.

A word I used more than others when referring to Vale.

My boy got antsy and wiggled his hips.

"All right, all right, I can take a hint."

I drew back and thrust in, canting my hips with each thrust until I hit his prostate. Into a punishing rhythm I went, one that sent my boy over the top as I relentlessly pounded that magical spot. Thank the orgasm gods for that because I hung on by a thread that snapped at the same time his did.

"Daddy!" he cried out as warm come spread between us.

His channel clamped my cock, and I was lost to the orgasm.

My sweet boy's barely audible, "I love you," before he drifted off sent me into a pleasant slumber. We napped for some time and woke in desperate need of a shower.

"Daddy, if you keep kissing me like that we'll never get cleaned up." A half-hearted protest if I ever heard one.

Somehow, my dick was magically on board for a round two which was oddly fast for me. "We forgot to try the plug."

Vale giggled. "Naughty Daddy."

"Let me get the water going." A quick press of lips to his temple and I hopped out of bed to start the shower.

The shower resulted in another orgasm and had the water not run cold we'd probably still be in there.

"Daddy, I'm hungry."

"Me, too, Little Monkey." Thankful I was that I'd stocked up before he came home. "Let's see what's in the cupboards."

Vale opened the dresser drawers until he found what he wanted and put on one of my T-shirts. Had we not had as many conversations as we did while he was at sea, our evening would have been awkward. Instead, it was perfect. Vale was comfortable at my place, something that normally would've taken time here to achieve, but I was glad that hadn't happened.

I slid into a pair of lounge pants, and gave his naked ass a playful tap as I passed him and raced him to the kitchen.

"Daddy!" He giggled and threw his arms around my neck. "That was naughty."

"There's more where that came from, cheeky boy."

Sexy, funny, playful, and he was all mine. I'd won the boyfriend lottery.

"How do omelets sound?" It was nearly sunrise so why not have breakfast before bed?

"Perfect. I'm not picky so whatever toppings you have are good for me." Vale sat on the nearby counter, sneaking bell peppers as I chopped then while I in turn stole kisses.

With full stomachs and far too many yawns, we curled up in bed with not a single plan for the rest of the day.

"This is nice, Daddy. I'm never gonna want to go home." He twirled my chest hairs between his nimble fingers.

"Then don't." Hell, if I had my way I'd have brought his luggage straight here rather than unloading it at his mother's house.

"You really mean that, don't you?"

"Never been more serious in my life. We spent the last three plus months getting to know one another and falling in love. Moving in together is the next step for us. Come with me this weekend to Whidbey and meet my parents."

He stared at me for a few seconds and said nothing. My gut wrenched and I feared I'd blown it.

"Okay."

"Okay?" I nearly blurted out about the land I'd bought after my last visit but decided in this case showing would be far more beneficial than telling.

"Yes, I'd like to meet them. They were so funny during our phone call." Vale yawned.

"Time for sleep, we can make all the arrangements when we wake. I love you, Vale, so fucking much."

"I love you, too, Daddy."

We woke sometime later to my phone ringing. "It's my mother," I held the phone up and Vale snagged it from me. He hit facetime and answered it.

"There's the sweet boy I was hoping to see. Welcome home, world traveler."

"Hello, Linda, I'm so happy to be back."

"It's like I don't even exist," I mock pouted.

"Is that my son whining beside you?"

Vale turned the phone so Mom could see my face. "Sure as hell is, Linda."

"Don't you Linda me, boy. Are you brining my new son out to visit this weekend?"

Vale's eyes lit up and his head bobbed away. Mom caught part of that and laughed. "Seems as though we will be gracing you with our presence."

"Good. Now, what are you two doing in bed at four o'clock in the afternoon?" She paused, obviously realizing what she'd asked. "Never mind, don't answer that." I heard my dad laughing in the background. "Saturday then?"

"Yes, Saturday for sure. I can't wait to finally meet you, Linda." Vale's smile was amazing and lit up everything inside of me. The way he and my mother connected only served to elevate our relationship.

"Same, Vale. Okay, make sure my son feeds you and we'll see you both then."

Vale ended the call. "You heard her, Daddy, you have to feed me."

Sadly, after dinner, I had to bid my boy farewell. He wanted to spend time with his mother, which after four months away I more than understood.

"What are you doing here? Isn't Vale back?" Diana hit me up as soon as I walked into the office.

"He is but he's spending some time with his mom. Figured I was better off here than at home moping around." That was putting it mildly. How did I go from happy bachelor to depressed as fuck after only being with my boy for twenty-four hours?

"Awe, our little Jackson is all growed up and in wove." Her use of the baby word for love only pissed me off, albeit briefly. Diana was like a sister to me, and I couldn't stay mad at her for long.

"Yeah, yeah, yeah. Bite me."

She threw her head back and laughed. "Your schedule is free for the rest of the week."

"Thanks. Taking him to meet the parents this weekend."

You could've heard a pin drop. That one line silenced her and as far as I knew, nothing before ever had.

"The fish look is not becoming on you, Diana." Open mouth, close mouth, open mouth, pause, close mouth. *Ah, it's open again and here it comes...*

"Holy shit. That's a big deal, Jack."

"Feels like the right deal. Besides, my mom already likes him better than me."

"Highly unlikely. Stop pouting, it's not becoming on you."

"Says who?"

"Says me."

It was like arguing with a sibling for which I had zero.

"Remind me again why I hired you."

"Because I won't take any shit from you."
"Hmm, sounds about right."

Chapter Fourteen
Vale

"Daddy!" I ran down the steps to him as he got out of the car. "I missed you."

"I missed you, too, Little Monkey. How's Mom?"

So silly, we talked multiple times these past couple of days and he knew how she was. "I think she's out of her gangster thug phase. Thank the reality TV gods for that one." I'd tried to research how to block certain channels from view but gave up about ten minutes into it. Attention span of a popsicle stick and all of that.

"Let's grab your bag and say goodbye."

We stepped back inside and there sat Mom, coffee in hand, buried in one of those damn shows. "Mom, Jack's here."

"Why hello, Daddy."

Just. Bury. Me. Now.

"Mom, really?"

She and Jack both laughed. I, on the other hand, was appalled.

"She's just having fun, Monkey. It's all good. Sarah, do you need anything before we hit the ferry?" Daddy was so sweet, always taking care us.

"No, but thank you for asking, Jack. You boys have a nice weekend." Mom gave us each a hug then Daddy carried my bag to the car and loaded it in by his.

"Okay, Monkey. You're in charge of the radio so dazzle me with your musical selections."

Daddy pulled out of the driveway and headed toward Mukilteo where we'd catch the ferry. We sang along with the show tunes, my favorites from Cabaret and even the Lion King came on. Before long we drove onto the ferry and once parked headed out onto the upper deck.

"It's been forever since I've ridden a ferry." A clear day in Seattle was rare yet we were granted one today. As I gazed out at the sound, Daddy wrapped his arms around me.

"I love this. Have you ever been to Orcas Island or seen the real orcas in the sound before?" Daddy asked.

"No, only on TV." It was rare we ever had the money to do much of anything and even though a drive to watch them while in the harbor was basically free, Mom usually had to work at the times they were here. A teacher's salary left a lot to be desired, especially considering all they did to help the kids they taught.

"We'll have to go someday. They're amazing." The captain's announcement came on to make our way back to the vehicles. Even though the ride was too short, I was excited to get back on the road.

Daddy rolled the top down on his convertible Mustang as we drove out of the ferry onto the main road on the island. The weather was perfect as was the company. No reason to fill the air between us with mindless chit chat when instead we soaked up this beautiful day with the wind whipping through our hair.

When the big red barn from my childhood memory came into view, I excitedly cheered. "Look, Daddy, it's still here." Imagine my surprise when he pulled in and parked.

"Yes silly boy, I sent you a picture of it when I was last here. Greenbank Farm is a Whidbey Island staple. Come on, Little Monkey, let's go inside."

Daddy came around and opened the door for me. "The swing set is still here. Do you think I could swing on it?" I hoped I wasn't too big to fit.

"If I didn't know any better, I'd say my monkey has a little side, too," Daddy winked. "Time to swing."

My laughter filled the air as Daddy pushed me on the swing. "Higher!" Once I was on a good roll, Daddy moved off to the side and took pictures of me.

"Silly Monkey, let's go inside and shop." Daddy helped me slow down enough so I could jump off. "Tens all across the board from the judges on that dismount. Good job. Now, let's take a selfie with the barn behind us." Daddy snapped a few more pictures, gave me a kiss, and then hand in hand we went on our next adventure.

"Gosh, nothing has changed since I was here." The large area you could rent for parties had the same tables and chairs inside and the restaurant area was just as quaint as I'd remembered. The wine tasting area was the first thing we saw when we walked in, but my mother wasn't a drinker, so we hadn't spent any time in that area before. Daddy sampled a couple of different wines and purchased them before we went into the café for lunch.

"I'm so full, I can't eat another bite." The sandwich and chips I had were wonderful but huge.

"Same. Let's walk next door and get some cheese. I always bring new ones for my parents to try."

Cheese and wine in hand, we were back on the road but a short drive later we pulled up in front of his parents' house. Daddy barely shut the engine off when Linda and Jackson came out to greet us.

"There's my new son!" She hugged me so hard it stole my breath.

"Mom, let him breathe."

"I'm just so excited. Jackson has never brought anyone home before."

This was gonna get confusing with Jackson being both Daddy's and his dad's name.

"Come on," Linda looped her arm through mine, "let them get the luggage. I've made raspberry lemonade."

"Yum. Raspberry anything is my favorite."

"Lord, help us," I heard Daddy's dad say. Geez, that was just as confusing as the two Jacksons deal.

"I love your home." This place was massive. "Oh my gosh, is that the water?" Standing just inside the entryway had a great view of the sound. Hell, the entire space had a fantastic water view.

"Yes, much like what Jackson did with his condo, we built this house with the water as the focal point and minimal interior walls to block it."

She sat the pitcher of lemonade and four glasses with ice on a tray and we took it out on the back deck. "Wow. This is nothing short of amazing."

"Glad to hear you like it." Daddy walked up beside me and kissed the top of my head.

We chatted for a while then Daddy said he wanted us to go for a walk. We strolled hand in hand along the shoreline. I could seriously stare out at this view for hours on end.

"This is where I always come when I need to clear my head and figure things out," Daddy said. "There's something about the water that sooths my soul."

"It's doing the same for me. It's like the weight of the world has been lifted. This place is beyond words." I couldn't imagine being able to afford to live here.

"Glad to hear you say that. When I was here last, missing my sweet boy, I made a lot of decisions."

"Decisions?"

"Yes, decisions that affect us."

I stopped, not wanting to veer too far off course in case I was dumped. Harder to call an Uber with no service. "How so?"

"I bought this land we're standing on."

"Um, what?" How did that affect us?

"I want us to build the house of our dreams on it."

"Um, what?" I'd turned into a parrot and a brainless one at that. "A house? For us?"

"I want us to design and build the house of our dreams and live in it together. Forever." Daddy was nervous and I was in shock. "I know it's fast and I'm not trying to scare you off, but I want a future with you. We can build a separate house for your mom and live our dream here, on the island."

When I didn't reply, he rambled on.

"We could build a gym so your monkey can climb away, and I can have a space in it to work out while you do your thing. We can even make a playroom that you and Darcy can use when she comes to visit."

"What about work? Where will I get a job?" There wasn't much around us. I supposed I could see if the little red barn was hiring.

"Honestly, if you don't want to work, you don't have to. But if you do," he quickly amended, "that is completely your choice. I just want to be with you. Always. Go to sleep with you, wake up with you. Spend the rest of my life with you."

Was that a proposal?

Had I been transported to an alternate universe where everything I'd ever dreamed of was handed to me? There had to be a flipside, right? For every positive came a negative and all that shit.

"I–I don't know what to say." Quite literally, to be honest.

"You don't have to say anything, and I didn't mean to freak you out." Daddy was sad, and that made me sad.

"Daddy, I love you. It's just...a lot and you surprised me is all." Okay, words were good. Communication was helpful. "Have you already started the whole building stuff?" I really had to get the correct lingo down before we embarked upon this adventure. Wait, was I in? My thoughts were a jumbled mess of what the fucks and time was what I needed to get them sorted.

"I've talked to an architect I've worked with on other projects who has agreed to take this one on. No rush. I told him what I envisioned but that nothing happened until I talked to you. You have just as much input on this design as I do."

"I–I," again with the stuttering. *Way to sound mature, Vale.* "I can't afford this. I don't have a job, or savings, or anything to contribute to it."

Daddy gently gripped my shoulders. "Deep breath, sweet boy. I don't mean to overwhelm you. Money is not an issue, our current and future needs come first. If it helps soothe you, think of it as an investment. You don't need to supply any capital, neither does your mother. Honestly, I love the idea of being able to take care of both of you. If you want to work, then do so. If you want to take online classes, then do so. If you want to run around in your monkey suit all day, then do so. The point is this is all up to you and you don't have to decide right this moment."

"To us. This is all up to us. I appreciate that you want to take care of me and Mom but it's just a lot to think about." I glanced out at the water as the sun began to set. I already knew my answer but had the sudden urge for a mother-son conversation prior to giving it.

"Take your time," Daddy pressed his lips to my forehead. "I'm not going anywhere."

"Hey, next weekend do you and Darcy want to go to Blush?" Daddy sprang on me as we walked back toward his parents' house.

"Darcy, too? Doesn't she have to be a member first?"

"I know the owner," Daddy winked. "Full disclosure, I'm a silent partner, in finance only, at Blush. But please, keep that to yourself."

Wow, he wasn't kidding when he told me he was invested in other non-start-up businesses.

"So, I know the owner and I can assure you it's okay. Based upon what you've shared with me about her life, I think she'd have fun playing with other littles."

"She would love that." I fired off a text to her about it.

Before we reached the house she replied.

I turned the screen toward Daddy so he could read it and he smiled. "I'll make all the arrangements."

The rest of the weekend was spent relaxing. Daddy and I took his parents' boat out and had a day out on the sound. It was hard to leave at the end of our trip and Linda made me promise to come back soon. For the drive home, we took the long way around, across Deception Pass and up through Anacortes.

"You're awfully quiet over there, Vale."

Vale. He hadn't called me that since we first started dating.

"Just have a lot on my mind."

"Oh. Anything I can help with?"

How do you tell someone you love that they're the one that sent your mind into overdrive without it sounding bad? "No, but thank you for asking."

Daddy kissed me goodnight at the door after carrying my bag inside then he left. Things were off with us, and I hated that. He offered me the dream of a life and I panicked.

"All right, Vale," Mom crossed her arms. "Spill it."

And so, I did. I told her everything about the house and working and how Daddy offered to include her in all of it.

"I don't know what to do." My brain was a murky mess and Mom always found a way to help me work past the sludge. I needed her enlightening words now more than ever.

"I was in love once, with your father. Only he didn't feel the same way." She sat beside me on the couch. "Sadly, he shared that with me when I told him I was pregnant."

"Mom, I'm so sorry." I couldn't imagine the heartbreak she felt.

"I was twenty, he was much older than me and he was married and one of my college professors. I didn't know about his marriage, or I never would've given him the time of day, but

I found out once it was too late. Since I was a little girl my only dream was to become a mother. I loved children and when I found out I was pregnant I was elated."

"Mom, I never knew."

"Of course you didn't, I refused to ever give you a reason to think you were a burden. You, my love, are a blessing. My one true gift in life. I finished college and got my degree before you came along. The moment I saw you everything in my world felt right. I didn't need a partner. I would make it on my own and give you the best life I could."

"Mom." Tears streamed down my face as I pictured a much younger version of my mother working hard while taking care of a baby by herself. This woman was made of much stronger material than I'd given her credit for.

"Vale, all I've ever wanted for you was for you to be happy. Jackson makes you happy. That man looks at you like you're made of gold. If he is offering you the life you want, a life with him where you will never want for anything again, you'd be a fool to deny yourself that."

"What about you, Mom? We're a team."

"My sweet baby boy. You have a heart that's made of that very gold that Jackson sees. You need to start your life together, just the two of you. I appreciate the offer to live there with you both, but I still have a few more years before I can retire. Maybe then I will reconsider but for now, it's your time to start your life. You can't stay home and look after your reality TV-addicted mother. I promise you I will be just fine."

"I love you, Mom."

"I love you, too, Vale. Now go get your man."

Chapter Fifteen
Jack

I'd just sat down, stiff drink in hand, when there was a knock at the door. "Hi."

"Vale, what are you doing here? Are you okay? Is Sarah okay? Please, come inside." Every question tumbled out with no break between.

"Daddy, I owe you an apology."

"You owe me no such thing, sweet boy."

"I do. You opened your heart and your dreams to me and I just...froze."

"It was a lot all at once and I got ahead of my-self. I didn't mean to scare you off." Fuck, had I ruined the best thing that'd ever happened to me? Always in forward motion I was, thinking of myself and my wants when I should've asked Vale first.

"You didn't scare me off. I'm here now, aren't I?"

"Yes, but the question is why?" Though I wasn't sure I'd like his answer.

"Okay, this isn't going the way I expected." Vale drew in a deep breath. "Sit."

I wasn't sure if it was the command in his voice or the serious look on Vale's face, but I did as he ordered even though I was supposed to be the Daddy here.

He paced a couple of times in front of the windows before he finally came to a stop. "I had a very interesting conversation with my mom when I got home. Learned a lot of things I didn't know about a father I never met." He shook his head. "Sorry, veered off course. Long story short, I want all the same things that you do, and I want them with you. The house, the life, marriage—the whole enchilada, but you blindsided me with it and I guess I just had to take a step back and assess it. And talk to my mom."

"Come here, sweet boy." I patted my lap, and he curled right up. Fuck, to think I almost lost this, or so I had thought. "I'm sorry, that wasn't my intention. I want to build a life with you, when you're ready. From now on when I go too fast, tell me to take it down a notch and I will. I love you more than anything in the world, Vale."

"I love you, too, Daddy, and I don't ever want to be without you."

In the back of my mind, this was a good idea, though it too could go horribly wrong.

"Good evening, Darcy. How are you today?" Vale and I had just shown up at her house to take her to Blush with us.

"I'm good, Daddy Jack. I've got my bag. I'm ready to go." Already slipping into little space it seemed as she took my hand and walked to the car with us. This bit of information gave me ideas for the playroom I wanted to build for her and Vale and future gifts for Darcy.

"I like your backpack. Are you a little princess?" Vale asked her and she nodded. "It's sparkly and I like the big silver tiara on top."

"Thank you. I like your monkey bag," she giggled. "It fits you perfectly."

These two were adorable. We'd not even made it to the club yet and I couldn't wait to see them play. I knew at some point my cheeky boy would veer away from the pet play area and wind up in the littles' room with his friend. I bet the other littles would love that. Silly monkey.

"All safe," I buckled them both into the back seat as neither wanted to be separated. They were so cute, holding hands and grinning wide-eyed up at me.

We arrived before the club opened and came in through the employee entrance at the rear of the building then walked toward the front where Vivienne's office was.

"Knock, knock," I called out at the open door and peeked my head inside. "Open to guests?"

"Always. It's wonderful to see you, my friend," Vivienne said as we embraced. "I'm dying to meet the boy who stole my best friend's heart."

"Hi," Vale peeked around me. "I'm Vale."

"Vale," Vivienne hugged him. I loved how personable my dear friend was. Don't get me wrong, cross her and you'd pay a hell of a penance. Her inner Domme took no shit. "I can't believe you tamed the bachelor's heart but given how adorable you are, I can see why. And who is this little one?"

Showtime.

Let's see if my feeble attempt at matchmaking worked.

"Ms. Vivienne, this is Vale's best friend, Darcy." I forgot to ask if she used a different name as a little, something to remedy later.

"Hello, Princess. It's wonderful to meet you." Vivienne extended her hand to Darcy. Vale still protectively held Darcy's other hand. Curiously, Darcy assessed Vivienne before reciprocating and I wondered if my forethoughts of a possible connection had been incorrect.

"I'll take them to the changing room and get them ready. I'll bounce between the playroom and pet area." Vivienne nodded though her eyes hadn't moved from Darcy. Did they already know each other? What was I missing here?

Darcy waited in the hall while I changed Vale then took her turn in the room. When she reappeared, she took my free hand as Vale held the other and together we went to the littles' room first.

"Squee!" One of the littles in the room squealed and ran toward us. "Look, Daddy, a monkey."

"My monkey," Darcy said rather firmly.

"Be nice, little one," I warned her, though not as firmly as she'd claimed Vale.

"Is that your Daddy?" another pointed to me and asked. "Do we have to ask him if we can play with your monkey?"

"What do you think, Little Monkey? Do you want to play with the littles tonight?"

Vale glanced from me to Darcy. Insecurity marred her adorable face, and I knew he wouldn't leave her alone. "Yes, please, Daddy," he whispered.

Hand in hand, Vale and Darcy walked to the center of the room where a handful of littles stood, waiting for the silly monkey to pounce. My boy was such a sweetheart and in no time he chased the giggling littles around the room. He'd drop on the floor and roll over and they'd try to catch him. With no obstacle courses in here, he sure had found another way to entertain the crowd and himself.

"He's perfect for you." My friend's sultry voice drew me from the hilarious scene.

"More than you know. What do you think of Darcy?" I had to ask. The suspense was killing me.

"Ah, I wondered how long it would take for you to ask. I see what you're up to, but I can't deny there is just something about her." Vivienne's gaze was on Darcy the entire time we spoke.

Darcy's head popped up as if she'd heard her name and she wobbled over to us and tugged at Vivienne's skirt. "Will you be my Mommy?"

I'd never witnessed a Domme, well, this Domme, stunned silent before as it took her a few moments to answer.

"Yes," Vivienne finally replied, took Darcy's hand and together they went to the reading nook.

My sweaty monkey appeared, having freed himself from the littles pile "Daddy, did you do this?"

"Mayyybbbeee."

Vale laughed. "I think Darcy's okay with us going to the pet room now."

I smiled as I watched Darcy sit in front of the chair Vivienne had claimed, the book Darcy had picked in hand, ready to read to what I hoped was her new girl.

"I think so, too, my love."

The pet room was full of wild animals, literally. There was no rock wall, though I'd be adding one soon along with a rope area where my monkey and others could swing. Vale stood beside me, taking it all in until a rogue puppy appeared at his feet.

"Hello, pup," I said, and he barked. "You want to play with my monkey?"

Bark. Bark.

"What do you say, Monkey? Care to entertain the pup?"

Vale's head bobbed. The pup ran out and came back when Vale hadn't moved and barked at him.

"Better go, Monkey. I don't think your new friend cares to wait any longer."

I watched as the pup led my monkey into the waiting group of new friends. Pups, kittens, another silly ferret, or perhaps the same one from the ship. Now that I thought about it, many of these costumes were familiar so I bet these were old friends Vale didn't realize he'd made.

The other handlers/Daddies and I gathered, chatting about our pets and come to find out, these were some of the same pets from the cruise. What a wonderful world my monkey and I had come into. Play dates were arranged and before I knew it, the time had come for the club to close for the night.

We gathered in the lobby, exchanging numbers and what not. Darcy joined us and as security locked the door, Vivienne emerged from her office.

"Did everyone have fun tonight?" she asked.

"Yes!" Vale energetically answered, though how he still had any energy at all I'd never know. I was worn out just from watching him. "My new friends are the same ones I played with on the cruise. This is so awesome!"

Vivienne smiled. "I'm so happy to hear that, Little Monkey."

"Are you ready to go, Darcy?" Vale asked her and Darcy stared wide-eyed up at Vivienne.

"I'll see to it she gets home safely," Vivienne smirked.

"Ah, indeed you will, my friend." I hugged her as Darcy and Vale did the same, though I did hear Vale whisper, "I'm so happy for you, Darcy. I love you."

"I love you, too, Vale."

My heart was near bursting and my smile wider than ever. Not only had I found the love of my life but it appeared my best friend, and Vale's, too, may have found theirs as well.

About TL Travis

TL Travis is an award–winning published author of LGBTQIA+ contemporary and paranormal romance, and erotic musings that have earned "Best–Selling Author" flags in the US as well as Internationally.

In her free time, TL enjoys catching up with her family, attending concerts, wine tasting, and traveling.

TL is surrounded by her extensive 4-legged rescue pets and growing family. She will continue saving furry friends in need for as long as she lives. Tl would like to remind you to "Adopt, not shop." Saving that lost soul may be just what you need.

https://linktr.ee/TLTravis

Also by TL Travis

The Social Sinners Series:

Boxset:

https://books2read.com/SSWorldTour

Behind the Lights, 1

MM Coming of Age Rockstar Romance

In the Shadows, 2

MM Rockstar Hurt/Comfort Romance

A Heart Divided, 3

MMM Rockstar Romance

Rhone's Rebel, 1
MM Hurt/Comfort Rockstar Romance
David's Disaster, 2
MM Daddy–boy Hurt/Comfort Rockstar Romance
Seltzer's Taylor, 3
MM Rockstar Romance
His Final Chase, 4
MM Rockstar Daddy-Little Romance
10/25/2024

Chaotic Abyss Series
Strike a Chord, 1
MM Rockstar Second Chance Romance

Daddies and their Littles
When Daddy Hurts
MM Daddy-Little Hurt/Comfort Romance
A Little Christmas: Jacob
MM Daddy-Little Hurt/Comfort Holiday Romance
A Little Christmas: Orion's Secret
MM Daddy-Little Hurt/Comfort Holiday Romance
A Daddy for Christmas: Brighton

MM Daddy Holiday Romance

Two Daddies for Henry

MMM Daddy Hurt/Comfort Found Family
Romance

A Little's Valentine's Party: Featuring Jacob &
Orion

Daddies and Littles Series

https://books2read.com/ALV

A Little's Valentine's Party: Featuring Jacob &
Orion

Daddies and Littles series

https://books2read.com/ALV

Pet Play

Pick Us, Daddy

Pride Pet Play 2023 Series

https://books2read.com/PPP2023

Ahoy Daddy!

Pride Cruise 2024 Series

MM Daddy Romance

Daddies:

Coming 8/16/24

Pints 'n Pool

Foggy Basin Series
MM Daddy Small Town Romance

<u>Standalone novels:</u>
Heat
MM Small Town Coming of Age Bear Bottom
Romance
See Me
MM Hurt/Comfort Enemies to Lovers Body
Positive/Disfigurement Romance

**<u>Greyson Fox Saga (each can be read as a
standalone):</u>**
Greyson Fox
MM Erotic May/December Age–Gap First
Time Coming of Age Romance
Forgive Me Father
MM Coming of Age Hurt/Comfort Rent–a–boy
Romance

<u>Stand–alone novelette's/novella's:</u>
Summer Boy
MM Small Town First-Time Coming of Age
Demisexual Romance
Girl Crush

MF (1 scene)/ FF Sapphic Romance
What Works For Us
FF Over 40 Erotic Novelette
Rules of the Game
MM Erotic Workplace Romance
Coffee, Tea or Me?
MM Contemporary Romance
Snowed In With You
MM Contemporary Second Chance Holiday
Romance

<u>**Paranormal Romance:**</u>
The Sebastian Chronicles
Historical Paranormal Erotic Romance
(Includes all 5 stories listed below)
Sebastian, The Beginning
MF Historical Paranormal Erotica
My Servant, My Lover
MF/MM Historical Paranormal Erotica
Wealthy Ménage
MF/MM/MFM/Ménage Historical Paranormal Erotica
Prohibition Inhibitions
MF/MM/MMF/MFM/BDSM Historical
Paranormal Erotica

The Tryst – Chronicle Finale
MM Paranormal Erotic Romance
Pity the Living, Not the Dead
MM Paranormal First Time Dark Romance

MF Titles are published under Raven Kitts